MOUNTAIN JACK PIKE

BULLS EYE BLOOD

#10

Also by Robert J. Randisi

MOUNTAIN JACK PIKE

BULLS EYE BLOOD

#10

Robert J. Randisi

SPEAKING VOLUMES, LLC
NAPLES, FLORIDA
2013

Bulls Eye Blood #10

ISBN 978-1-61232-601-6

PROLOGUE

Cal Devers and Henri LeConte had several things in common that made them ideal partners. First, they were both trappers and hunters, and had been for years.

Calvin Devers was forty-five, and had been hunting and trapping in the Rockies for thirty-five of them. He had always been a loner, until he met LeConte about five years ago.

Henri LeConte was thirty-eight, but he had come to the United States from his native France when he was very small, and had found himself alone in the Rockies at the tender age of fourteen, when his entire family was killed by Indians. He had been on his own since that time, hunting and trapping to live, until he met Calvin Devers.

Both Devers and LeConte were very good at what they did, but there was something else they were both very good at.

Stealing.

It was only about a year after they became partners

that they decided there might be an easier way to make a living. Why not let others do the trapping and hunting, and then steal from them? They tried it once, and it was so easy—and profitable—that they had been doing it ever since.

At the moment they were looking down at a camp from a ridge high above it, and they both had visions of their biggest haul yet.

"How many of them do you figure there are?" Devers asked LeConte.

"I bet you got forty hunters down there, with their families."

"That's a lot of hunters," Devers said. He looked at his partner with a sly grin and added, "That makes for a lot of hides."

"*Oui, mon ami,*" LeConte said, "and a lot of profit for us, eh?"

Both men laughed.

"When do you think we should take them?" LeConte asked Devers. The American was the planner of the two.

"June rise is comin' up," Devers said. The June rise was when the melting snow coming down from the mountains caused the level of the Missouri River to rise. "I bet they decide to take the skins downriver by boat."

"They will never get a steam-powered boat up here," LeConte said.

"No," Devers said, "but they can build themselves some mackinaws."

LeConte rolled his eyes and said, "Dat is a lot of work, no?"

"That is a lot of work, yes," Devers said, "but they're

gonna be doin' it, not us."

Both men laughed again.

"Dat means they are weeks away from transporting the skins," LeConte said. "What are we supposed to do in the meantime?"

"We do what we do best, Henri, my friend," Devers said, smiling. "We wait."

Indeed, they had become very good at waiting, because waiting for the right time was often the key to successfully stealing another hunter's skins.

"There is only one small problem that I can see," Devers said, staring down at the camp.

"What is dat?"

"Look there . . . near the stream. The bare-chested man." The stream was actually a tributary of the great Missouri.

LeConte looked and saw what the man Devers was indicating. He was very tall, perhaps even six-and-a-half feet tall, and well muscled. He had a full head of hair, and a full beard. At the moment, he seemed to be bathing.

"Is dat who I think it is?" LeConte asked. The Frenchman was not a tall man, standing only about five foot eight. Nor was he powerfully built. Consequently, he was impressed by men who were both.

"Yeah," Devers said, distaste plain in his voice, "that's Jack Pike."

"What is Pike doing here?" LeConte asked. "He usually hunts alone."

"Or with Skins McConnell," Devers said. "I see McConnell down there, too."

"*Mon ami,*" LeConte said, "stealing from Jack Pike, dat is not a healthy thing to do." His tone also betrayed him, but in his case what he was feeling was great discomfort and doubt.

"He's just a man, Henri," Devers said. "No different from you and me."

Devers stood over six feet, but he was a slender man. Rather than be in awe of men like Pike, however, he envied them and, because of that, hated them. Jack Pike, because of his stature—both physical and that of his reputation—he hated most of all.

"Tell that to the Indians," LeConte said. "No matter what the tribe—Crow, Blackfoot, Dakota, whatever—they call him He-Whose-Head-Touches-The-Sky. And the white men call him a legend, like Jim Bridger."

"If it was Bridger down there I'd have second thoughts," Devers said, although that wasn't quite true, "but I am not about to pass up this haul just because Jack Pike is down there." He looked at his partner and said in a tone designed to tweak his ego, "If you're not with me on this one, Henri, let me know, while I have time to get someone else."

"No, no," LeConte said, "that will not be necessary, *mon ami*. I am with you . . . if you really think we can do it."

"We can do it," Devers said, "we'll just have to get some help, that's all."

To himself he added, A lot of help.

CHAPTER ONE

It surprised even Jack Pike himself that he and Skins McConnell had become part of Harley Rose's camp. Pike and McConnell had ridden up on Rose's camp in mid-February, and had accepted an invitation to stay for a few nights. It was now almost June, and they were still there.

Of course, Pike knew that for McConnell part of the incentive was a tall, willowy blonde named Sheila. Their eyes had met almost the moment they had ridden into camp, and by that night McConnell was sharing her tent—and her bedroll.

For his own part, a tall, heavy-breasted, black-haired gal named Rita made his nights bearable, but unlike McConnell and Sheila, he and Rita had not hit it off immediately. . . .

When Pike and McConnell came within sight of the camp they debated whether or not they should ride around it, avoiding it.

"It looks like a big camp," McConnell said, "and we're short of supplies."

"All right, then," Pike said, "we'll ride in and see if we can buy some supplies from them . . . but then we ride right back out again. Deal?"

"Deal."

As soon as they rode into town, however, Pike and McConnell saw the tall blond woman, and Pike saw the look that passed between her and his friend—and then, of course, there was Harley Rose.

Rose was a big barrel-chested man with a perpetually good humor. He was in his late forties, with gray streaking the black of his hair and beard.

"Pike? Jack Pike, is that you?"

"Harley?" Pike replied.

As Rose approached him Pike stepped down from his horse. The two clasped hands and shook vigorously. Pike was several inches taller than Rose, but the other man's hand was every bit as big as his own.

"It's been a long time," Rose said.

"Two or three years, I guess."

"More like four."

McConnell dismounted and took his eyes off the woman long enough to meet Rose.

"Harley, this is Skins McConnell."

McConnell shook hands with Rose, and then his eyes slid over to the woman again. She was standing off to one side, presiding over a steaming pot. She was wrapped well against the cold, but even so he could see that she was handsomely formed.

"What are you and your friend up to?" Rose asked.

"Well, we were hunting, but we ran low on supplies," Pike said.

"It's not like you to plan poorly."

10

"I didn't," Pike said. "We ran into some Crow and had to trade some of our supplies."

"A big band?"

"Big enough to make us decide to trade rather than fight."

"Well," Rose said, "let me have your horses taken care of, and then we can get some hot food and coffee into your bellies. After that, we'll see what we can do about outfitting you."

"We just need enough supplies to get us to Kennedy's Hole, where we can outfit completely."

"Nonsense," Rose said, "we can fix you up right here. Come on."

Rose called over a man who walked off with their horses, then led Pike and McConnell over to the fire where the blond woman was standing.

"Sheila, how about some of that stew for our guests?" Rose asked.

"That depends," Sheila said, "on who our guests are, Harley?"

"Ah, my bad manners are betrayin' me again," Rose said, chiding himself. "Sheila, this is Jack Pike, and that's Skins McConnell. Boys, meet Sheila Chapin. She does most of our cookin' around here, which is why we got ourselves such a big camp. Hunters come from all over to sample Sheila's cookin'."

"Is that true?" McConnell asked.

"Every word," Sheila said. "I'll give you each a bowl and you can decide for yourselves."

She did just that and both men had to admit that what Harley Rose had said was probably true. They hadn't tasted anything so good in a long time.

11

"Wait until you try her coffee," Harley Rose said. "Hey, Sheila, how about a bowl for me?"

"Coming up, Harley."

After she handed him a bowl the three of them found a place to sit not far from the fire, but out of Sheila's hearing range.

"Is she, uh, yours?" McConnell asked.

"Sheila?" Rose said. "Nah, Sheila's on her own. There's been plenty of men wantin' to change that, but she ain't been ready. You interested?"

"We're supposed to be leaving soon," Pike said, eyeing his partner.

"I just want to get some more stew," Skins said, standing up.

Both Pike and Rose watched as McConnell walked over to the fire and started talking to the blond woman.

"I guess he's interested," Rose said.

"I guess so."

That was when Pike saw the dark-haired woman. She was a distance away, but his eyes were good enough to notice her. A man would have had to be totally blind not to notice her. She was a big woman, full-bodied, in her thirties. At the moment she was doing laundry. She looked up at that moment, though, and caught him looking at her. She held his eyes boldly for a long few moments, then looked back to her work.

"Tell me about those Crow Indians. Any chance they'll come this way?"

"It's possible," Pike said, taking his eyes off the woman, "but I don't think you'll have to worry about them. There was only about a dozen. How many men do you have here?"

12

"We're about forty hunters, plus family—some of whom can shoot. Take Sheila, for instance. She can shoot almost as good as she can cook."

"If she could shoot as good as she looks she'd be dangerous," Pike said. "I don't think you have anything to fear from a dozen Crow braves."

"Not unless they get themselves some reinforcements," Rose pointed out.

"Well," Pike said, putting down his empty bowl, "if we can get some supplies from you we'll be on our way."

"Coffee first," Rose said. "Rita!"

Pike looked up and saw the dark-haired woman passing by. She responded to her name by looking over at Pike and Harley Rose.

"How about gettin' a couple of cups of coffee from Sheila and bringin' them over here."

"What do I look like?" the woman demanded. "A waitress?"

"Come on, Rita—"

"Bad enough I got to do laundry," Rita said, "now they want waitress service—"

"Rita, we have guests."

"Guests?" she said. "Now we're a hotel?"

"Rita—"

"Never mind," she said. "I'll get you the coffee."

As she walked away Rose grinned and said, "Rita's a little difficult to get along with . . . sometimes . . ."

"Then it's a good thing I won't have to try," Pike said, "since we'll be moving along as soon as—"

"Let's talk about that," Rose said.

"About what?"

13

"About whether you should leave or not," Rose said. "Remember, there's a Crow huntin' party out there."

"Which we've already dealt with."

"Now, Pike," Rose said, "you know as well as I do that Indians don't always stay dealt with."

"That may be—"

"Look, your goal is the same as ours," Rose said. "To hunt and trap and make a livin'. Well, we can do it together."

"We can do it separately, too, Rose. You know I don't like to be around a lot of people—"

"There's safety in numbers, Pike—"

He stopped as Rita came over with the coffee.

"Here," she said, thrusting it at them.

"Thank you," Pike said, barely escaping a spill.

"You plannin' on stayin' here?" Rita asked.

Up close he could see that she wasn't as beautiful as Sheila, but there was something about her that attracted him more than the blond woman did—which was probably just as well, from the looks of the way Sheila and McConnell were talking.

"We're discussin' that now," Rose said. "Rita, this is Jack Pike."

"I heard of you," she said. "If you stay, don't be expectin' this kind of service all the time."

"I won't."

Rita nodded and walked away.

"Won't what?" Rose asked. "Stay, or expect that kind of service?"

"Either," Pike said, "or neither."

"Look," Rose said, leaning forward, "why not stay the night and think it over? Sheila will be cookin' dinner—"

14

"Harley—"

"How's the coffee?"

"The coffee is fine," Pike said. As a matter of fact, it was more than just fine. It was the best coffee he'd had in months. It might even have been good enough—the coffee *and* the stew—to stay overnight for.

"Then you'll stay?" Rose asked.

Pike studied him for a moment, then held out his coffee cup and said, "Just overnight."

Rose smiled, took the cup and said, "I'll get you some more coffee."

As Rose went for the coffee he passed McConnell on the way and they exchanged a few words. When McConnell reached Pike he was grinning.

"We're stayin'?" McConnell asked.

"Overnight," Pike said, again.

McConnell sat down next to Pike. He was holding a half-full coffee cup.

"Good coffee, huh?"

"Good coffee, good stew," Pike said. "I'll bet she's good at everything she does."

"I'll let you know," McConnell said, his grin widening, "in the mornin'."

There was more stew for dinner that first night, which suited Pike just fine. He ate it outside of Harley Rose's tent, while McConnell had his dinner sitting with Sheila.

"Your friend seems to have made an impression on Sheila," Rose said.

"He does that with women."

"Ain't never seen her pay that much attention to a

15

man before."

Pike looked into Harley Rose's eyes and said, "We're still leaving in the morning."

"You keep sayin' that," Rose said, "but I seen the way you looked at Rita."

"What?"

"And the way she looked at you."

"If you ask me," Pike said, "that's one female who doesn't like men."

"We'll see," Rose said, smiling, "we'll see."

After dinner Pike took a turn around camp with Rose and discovered that there were many hunters in camp he knew. Then again, you couldn't spend as many years in the mountains as he had, put forty hunters together in one place, and not come up with a good number you were acquainted with.

"Lots of folks here you know," Rose observed.

"Some."

"Could be a worse place to finish out the winter and do some spring huntin'," Rose said.

"Could be."

"Damn it, Pike—"

"Harley, now you know I like to hunt alone—"

"Or with McConnell?"

"One or two men, Harley, that's my preference," Pike said.

"I know that, Pike," Rose said, "but times is hard. This may be the only way to make one last big strike before the mountain runs dry of beaver and skins."

It was true that the beavers were becoming more and more rare. Pike had been seeing that for the past couple of years himself.

"Talk to your partner, Pike," Rose suggested, "and

see what he says."

Pike looked over at McConnell, who was still sitting with Sheila.

"I think I know what he'll say."

"Stay a week, Pike," Rose said, "then make up your mind."

"You're a persistent cuss, Harley."

"I'm bein' selfish, Pike," Rose said. "You're the best hunter in the mountains, and I'm the best trapper. I've got a nose for beaver, boy, and I know they're here. Between us we can really make a killin' here. It'll make the rest of the year some easier to get through."

Pike had to admit that Harley Rose had a reputation for knowing where the beavers were. If he and McConnell left in the morning Pike would feel bound and determined to leave the area. If he trapped beaver here, it would only be because he knew Rose was in the area, but to him that would be like poaching. If he stayed, though . . .

"All right, Harley," Pike said, finally. "I'll talk to Skins. We'll stay, maybe a week . . ."

"And maybe longer."

"Maybe," Pike said. "No promises, though."

"I'll make a promise," Rose said. "I'm gonna find so much beaver here that you won't be able to leave even if you want to."

Later, Pike approached McConnell with the idea of staying, and knew he wasn't going to have to do much convincing.

"It's all right with me," McConnell said, "but what about you, Pike? You don't usually like bein' around

17

this many people."

"Harley made a few good points, Skins," Pike said, "and I'm willing to give it a try . . . for a while, anyway."

"Well, like I said," McConnell repeated, looking over to where Sheila was standing, "It's all right with me."

"How did I know you were going to say that?"

CHAPTER TWO

True to his word Harley Rose had found beaver aplenty, and over the first week that Pike and McConnell were there the traps had yielded an abundance of beaver.

Similarly, the hunting proved to be plentiful, and there was certainly no good reason to leave at the end of the first week as far as the trapping and hunting were concerned.

Of course, McConnell had no good reason to leave, as the blonde Sheila had been sharing her tent with him since the first night.

Harley Rose had managed to find Pike an empty tent, so that the biggest man in camp wouldn't have to share one with anyone.

Pike's presence in camp was welcomed by most. There were only two people who really didn't seem thrilled that he was there. One of those was Rita, the buxom, dark-haired woman who, for some reason, seemed to resent his presence there.

The second person was a man named John Blackburn. Harley and the others called him "Blackie." Blackburn was in his late twenties, and stood six foot three. He had a huge, midnight black beard and, until Pike's arrival, he had held the distinction of being the biggest man in camp. That distinction seemed to mean something to him, and he didn't like losing it.

On the eighth day, as Pike had coffee with Harley Rose, Rose talked to him about Blackburn.

"The man is cut out of stone, Pike," Rose said, "and there ain't an ounce of fat on him. I ain't never seen his like when it comes to brute strength—unless maybe it's you."

"I'm not looking to match strength with anyone, Harley," Pike said, "and I don't like the way he looks at me, like he wants to test me."

"Oh, he does," Rose said. "He's just itchin' to test you, as a matter of fact."

"And how long have you known that?"

"Since the first day you rode in."

"And you still wanted me to stay?"

"Hey," Rose said, "if it came down to you or him in camp, I'd give him a horse and send him on his way without a second thought. Of course . . . I'd prefer to keep you both here."

"Keep him away from me," Pike said, "and we won't have a problem with that. Okay?"

"Fine by me," Rose said. "Now, what about Rita?"

"What about her?"

"Are you and her gonna get together, or what?"

"Harley," Pike said, "the woman hasn't spoken two civil words to me since we got here."

"That's just her way," Rose said. "She likes you, I can tell."

"Yeah, well, she's got a funny way of showing it," Pike said. "If looks could kill I'd be dead ten times over, already."

"Like I said," Rose said, "that's just her way. Give her a chance."

"Yeah," Pike said, "but if you don't mind, Harley, I don't think I'll be showing my back to her, or to Blackburn, either."

"Leave Blackie to me," Harley Rose said, "but Rita is your problem."

At that moment Rita passed by, without looking at Rose or Pike. Pike looked at her, though, and watching her walk past he figured that he'd had plenty of worse-looking problems in the past.

For weeks Pike and Rita exchanged nothing but glances. After a month—a month that sneaked right past Pike when he wasn't looking—Pike began to think that Harley Rose might be right.

She just might like him.

By talking to other people he had learned a little about Rita Macon. She had been married to a mountain man for five years, and then he suddenly left her. There were those who thought that he had gone hunting and been killed, but Rita insisted that he had simply left her, without a word. Since then—two years ago—she had nothing but distaste for men—a distaste bordering on hatred.

But maybe that was changing . . .

Pike had been involved with enough women over the years to know when one was interested in him, even if it was against her will.

*****

"So?" Pike said to McConnell.

"So . . . so what?" McConnell asked, giving his friend a puzzled look over his coffee cup.

"Are we here until spring?"

McConnell grinned.

"It's almost April, Pike," McConnell said. "You waited until now to ask me that?"

"How are things with you and Sheila?"

"There's another question you know you don't have to ask."

"I guess not. . . ."

"What's the matter, Pike?" McConnell asked. "Getting the urge to travel?"

Pike moved his shoulders, as if they were bearing some great weight, and said, "Too many people."

"I know what you need."

"What?"

"A woman?"

"And that would fix everything?"

"How are things between you and Rita?"

"There is nothing between me and Rita."

McConnell's grin widened and he said, "You mean nothing physical . . . yet."

"You're crazy."

"No," McConnell said, "you're going crazy." He leaned over and touched his friend's arm. "You need a woman, Pike. You need Rita."

"Maybe," Pike said, "but what does she think?"

"She thinks the same thing," McConnell said.

"How do you know?"

"Sheila and Rita are friends."

"So?"

"So, Sheila can see what Rita needs just like I can see what you need."

"You mean the two of you know what's good for us even if we don't?"

"Exactly."

"And is Sheila talking to Rita at this moment?"

"I don't know for sure," McConnell said, "that it's at this very moment. . . ."

Pike was reclining in his tent that night when he sensed someone right outside.

"Skins?"

There was no answer.

"Harley?"

Someone pushed the flap back, and Rita stuck her head inside.

"I'm sorry," she said, "I hope I'm not disturbing you."

"No," Pike said, "it's all right." He sat up on the pallet that had come with the tent and put his feet on the ground. "Uh, can I do something for you?"

"Can I come in?"

"Sure."

She entered, letting the flap fall closed behind her. She stood right there in front of the flap with her hands behind her back.

"What have you heard about me?" she asked.

Pike stared at her, and then decided to answer her honestly.

"Talk."

"You heard about my husband?"

"Yes."

"He left me," she said, "and I guess I been takin' out on all men."

Pike nodded, but didn't say anything.

"I guess I pretty much been takin' out on you most of all, lately."

"Have you? We haven't spoken much."

"That's what I mean," Rita said. "I snapped at you the first day you got here, and I guess I been givin' you a lot of dirty looks since then."

"Do I remind you of your husband?" Pike asked.

"No," she said, "just the opposite."

"But I'm a man."

"Yeah, right," she said.

"So you came over to apologize?"

"Yeah," she said, "I guess . . ."

"You guess?"

She brought her hands around in front of her and rubbed them together.

"I ain't been with a man since my husband left."

"That's a long time."

"Yeah, it is," she said. "The funny thing is, I ain't never *wanted* to be with a man since he left—until now, that is."

"Now?"

"Well . . . since you got here."

"Rita," Pike said, "are you saying—"

"I guess I shouldn't have come here," she said, flushing suddenly. "I didn't think—"

Pike stood up and walked toward her as she turned to the tent flap.

"Rita," he said, grabbing her arm. He didn't hold her tightly, but his grip was firm enough to stop her.

"Pike—"

He turned her to face him. This was the closest he'd been to her since arriving in camp. Her face had a strong bone structure. Firm jaw, full lower lip, strong cheekbones. He leaned down and kissed her on the mouth. At first she didn't respond, but then her mouth softened beneath his and she leaned into the kiss. He could feel her trembling, and he didn't know if it was from pent-up passion, or fear.

"Rita . . ."

"What?" she asked, her forehead pressed to his chest.

"Have you talked to Sheila lately?"

She looked up at him with eyes he just noticed were black and said, "How did you know?"

"Just a lucky guess."

She looked past him at the pallet.

"Do you think that will hold both of us?"

He turned and looked at it and said, "Well, if it doesn't, we can always use the floor."

Now it was almost June, and Pike and Rita had been sharing her tent for the past five weeks, because it was bigger than the one Rose had given to Pike.

This morning, Pike was once again experiencing surprise. Surprise that he and McConnell had ridden into Harley Rose's camp in February, and had stayed, and surprised that he was lying among half a dozen blankets with Rita Macon, after the reception he'd gotten from her that first day.

"What are you thinkin'?" she asked from behind him.

He turned and looked down at her. She was lying on

25

her back, her black hair fanned out behind her head. The blankets were up to her neck, but by now he knew the body beneath the blankets well. She was a big woman, with heavy breasts and thighs, and a nicely padded ass and belly. She wasn't one of those slender, small-breasted things who bruised easily. She was the kind of woman a man Pike's size needed.

"What are you thinkin' about?" she asked again.

"The mountains."

She sat up and the blanket fell away from her breasts. They were heavy, almost plump, with dark brown nipples that were puckering now against the cold.

"We're in the mountains."

"Now," he said, "I mean high up, where there's snow all the time and the water is ice cold."

"The water's cold here, too."

"Not like up there."

Suddenly, he felt her hand close on his upper arm. She had a strong grip and she was squeezing his right bicep.

"Are you thinkin' of leavin'?"

He looked at her and said, "Darlin', I've been thinking about that since I got here, haven't I?"

She released his arm now and slid her hand over his chest.

"And I've been tryin' to keep you from thinkin' it, haven't I?"

"And doing a good job of it, too," he said, as she slid her hand down over his belly and into his lap.

"So I see . . ."

He pushed her down on her back and pulled the blanket off her completely. He kissed her, long and lingeringly, and then ran his lips over her chin, her throat, her shoulders, and her breasts. He paused there to suck on her nipples and she moaned and gripped his hair with her hands. She writhed beneath him as he continued to nibble her breasts, and then he continued his downward path until his head was nestled between her meaty thighs. He worked furiously on her with his mouth and tongue until she was crying out and reaching for him. He mounted her and slid into her, groaning as her heat closed around him. . . .

John Blackburn sat in front of his tent, warming his hands around a cup of coffee. From where he was sitting he could see Rita Macon's tent, and he knew what was going on inside.

From the first day Pike had arrived in camp John Blackburn was an unhappy man. He knew Pike's reputation, but he did not respect the bigger man for it. One of the reasons, of course, was that Pike *was* a bigger man. Blackburn didn't like men who were bigger than he was. He thought that bigger men thought they were better than he was, and he had gone through his life thrashing them and showing them that they weren't.

The past three months had been unhappy ones for Blackburn. Harley Rose had warned him away from Pike, but for the past five weeks Pike had been sharing Rita's tent, and for that Blackburn hated him the most.

John Blackburn was in love with Rita Macon, and had been since the first time he saw her. She would have nothing to do with him—or with any man, for that matter, until Pike arrived. Still, he had always thought that he would eventually win her over. That wouldn't happen, though, with Pike around.

So every morning for the past five weeks Blackburn had been drinking his first cup of coffee out in front of his tent, watching Rita's and torturing himself by imagining what was going on inside.

He knew that just minutes from now Rita would be coming out of her tent. She would go over to one of the campfires, get two cups of coffee, and carry them back to the tent.

He watched, and waited.

CHAPTER THREE

From high above the camp Cal Devers watched the early morning goings-on with great satisfaction. He knew that the hunters in the camp had stockpiled a great deal of beaver, and an impressive cache of hides. He also knew—probably before they even knew it— that the only way for them to take the skins to market was by the river.

Devers was alone at the moment, but he knew that soon Henri LeConte would be returning with at least half a dozen men, maybe more. He himself had only just returned. Hell, there was no point in watching them for three months. He knew damn well that as May approached they'd still be here.

After LeConte returned, Devers would go out himself and get some real cheap help.

He knew some Crow Indians who would help them for nearly nothing. Some blankets and beads, maybe even some whiskey was all it would take.

LeConte was worried about the number of hunters there were in camp, but since Devers had no intention of attacking the camp, he wasn't worried about that. Once they loaded the skins onto boats there'd only be a handful to contend with.

It wouldn't be long now, at all. . . .

The mackinaws were Pike's idea.

It came one night, soon after he and McConnell decided to stay. He, McConnell, Rose, and several other men who made up the brain trust of the camp were sitting around a campfire, going over options for delivering their wares. John Blackburn was there, but was quiet.

"If we wait for the spring rise," Pike said, "we can take them by the river."

"We'd never get a steamboat up here," a man named Evans said.

"We could use keelboats," another man said.

"Keelboats would be too slow," Rose said.

"We can build mackinaws."

The mackinaw was clumsy, but effective, and continued to be used even after the steamboat was introduced to Missouri travel.

The mackinaw was a large, broad, flat-bottomed boat. The tops were covered with bent branches of trees, and then covered with waterproof buffalo hides. Each boat would have four oarsmen and a steerman, who would manage the boat by standing on a broad board. The helm would be ten feet long, and the rudder five or six feet long. Aided by the strong current of the Missouri, a mackinaw could cover as much as a hundred miles a day.

"How could we build mackinaws?" a man asked.

"We won't," Pike said, "not here. We'd send someone to Fort Pierre, upriver. They have a boatyard near there. If they started building them now, they'd be ready by the June rise."

"How many would we need?" Evans asked.

Pike looked at Rose and said, "How many hides do we have?"

"By June rise we'll have close to six thousand."

"We'd need at least two boats," Pike said. "Has anyone here ever worked a mackinaw?"

"I have," McConnell said.

So had Pike, and Rose said he knew of three or four other men in camp who had.

"That's fine," Pike said. "We can teach others so that they'll be ready by then."

"Where would we be taking the hides, then?" someone asked.

"St. Joe," McConnell replied, "or to St. Louis."

Pike made a face. He and McConnell had been in St. Louis once, and they'd had nothing but trouble.

"Wait a minute," Evans said. "Having these boats built is gonna cost money."

"Money that we'll get back," Pike said, "not only when we deliver our load, but when we reach St. Joseph or St. Louis we can sell the boats for firewood."

"When we reach our destination, we can offload the skins to a steamboat, or a barge."

"It sounds good to me," Harley Rose said. "What about the rest of you?"

There were still some arguments, but by the night's end they had agreed that the mackinaws were their best bet.

After the meeting broke up, Pike, McConnell, and Rose stayed to talk further.

"What remains now," Rose said, "are two things."

"Name 'em," McConnell said.

"First of all, who is going to go to the boatyard up near Fort Pierre and make arrangements for the mackinaws?" Rose said.

"That's easy," Pike said. "Skins and I will go."

"I had a feelin' you'd say that," Rose said. He knew that Pike was itchin' to get on horseback and get away from camp.

"Yeah," McConnell said, "so did I." McConnell wasn't so eager to leave camp. Pike wondered just how close his friend and Sheila really were getting.

"What's the second thing?" McConnell asked.

"Transporting the skins to the boatyard," Rose said.

"Do we have enough mules?" Pike asked.

"I'll have to check."

"If not, Skins and I can pick some up at Fort Pierre. By the time we're ready to move them, the camp'll be ready to break up. Some of us can start ahead with the skins, but the others can follow to Fort Pierre. That's as good a place to wait as any."

"All right," Rose said. He tapped Pike on the arm and said, "I knew havin' you here was a good idea."

"That makes one of us," Pike said.

Rose stood up and left to return to his own tent. The man had his own tent, and no companion to share it with. Pike was sure this was by choice.

"You had to volunteer us, didn't you?" McConnell asked when the other man was gone.

"Hey, I can go to Fort Pierre alone and arrange for the mackinaws," Pike said. "Stay here."

"No, no," McConnell said, "I'll go with you. I don't want you runnin' into a huntin' party all by yourself. You're not the trader I am."

"That's so true," Pike said.

"Well, you're not."

"I'm agreeing with you."

"When should we start?" McConnell asked.

"Tomorrow's as good a time as any."

"Yeah," McConnell said, standing up. "I better go and tell Sheila—and you better tell Rita."

Pike didn't anticipate this as a problem. He certainly had not become as attached to Rita as McConnell had to Sheila.

He watched his friend walk away, and decided to have another cup of coffee.

Starting up with Rita had seemed like a good idea at the time, but more and more he was starting to think that it had been a bad idea. She seemed to be obsessed with when he would be leaving, and whether or not he would come back. He knew he should have been honest—brutally honest—with her and told her that when he did leave, he wouldn't be coming back. None of them would. When the hunting was over and they were ready to transport their skins, the camp would be disbanded and everyone would go their own ways. The sooner she realized that, the better off they'd all be.

And he certainly wasn't prepared to take her with him when he left. He had already done that with one woman in his life, and the result had been disastrous. He wasn't about to repeat that mistake.

Early the next morning Pike met McConnell outside. McConnell had already saddled their horses.

"So?" McConnell said.

"So what?"

"How'd it go?"

"It went fine."

"No panic?"

"About what?"

"About maybe you leavin' and not comin' back?"

Pike paused as he was about to mount up and looked at McConnell.

"What did Sheila say to you?"

"Only that Rita was starting to worry that you'll leave her, like her husband did."

"Only?"

Pike mounted up and looked down at his friend.

"You know, it was your idea for me to take up with her."

McConnell mounted up and said, "Now you're blamin' me?"

"No," Pike said, "I'm blaming myself. When I heard those stories about her husband I should have forgotten about her."

"She's kind of hard to forget," McConnell said.

"I thought you liked your women thin and blond, like Sheila?" Pike asked.

"I do," McConnell said, "but that don't mean that Rita ain't hard to forget."

Pike shook his head and said, "The poor bastard."

"Who?"

"Rita's husband."

"Is she that bad?"

"No," Pike said, testily, "I don't mean that."

"Then why is he a poor bastard?"

34

"Because he's probably lying dead out there somewhere," Pike said, "and she's convinced that he left her."

"And you think you can convince her that he didn't?" McConnell asked.

"Oh, not me," Pike said. "That'd be up to her friends, like your Sheila."

"Sheila's tried."

McConnell looked back and saw Sheila standing in the open flap of her tent. She waved and he waved back. He looked over at Rita's tent then, and saw that she was not watching.

"Uh-oh," he said.

"What?" Pike asked.

"Looks like we got company," McConnell said, jerking his chin.

Pike looked and saw John Blackburn riding toward them. He and Blackburn had spoken very little during the time he'd been there. It looked like that was about to change.

"Headed somewhere in particular?" Pike asked.

"I'm goin' with you."

"Who says?" Pike asked.

"I do."

"You talk to Harley about this?"

"I don't need Harley's permission."

Pike was about to say, "But you need mine," when he stopped himself. If he didn't dislike the man—and if he wasn't sure that the feeling was returned—would he object to his accompanying them?

The answer was no. There was every likelihood of their running into Indians between here and Fort Pierre, and the more men they had with them the

35

better—especially a big man like John Blackburn. The Indians respected courage, but they also respected strength and size. Pike knew that Blackburn had two of those traits, but did he have the third?

"All right," Pike said, to McConnell's surprise. "If Skins has no objection, you can come along."

Blackburn looked at McConnell, who recovered from his surprise enough to say, "Uh, no, no, I don't have any objections."

"All right, then," Pike said, "let's get moving. We should be able to make Fort Pierre in two days."

"As long as we don't run into any trouble," McConnell said.

"Right," Pike said, "with no trouble."

As they rode out, single file, Pike thought, no trouble from the Indians, and no trouble between him and John Blackburn. Pike had no doubt that in a hand-to-hand situation he could defeat John Blackburn, but the man was big and strong—and young—and it just might be that he'd have to kill him to beat him.

He couldn't think of anything worth doing that over—not at the moment, anyway.

CHAPTER FOUR

They rode through the morning into the afternoon and stopped to give the horses a blow. Pike and McConnell had spoken several times during the ride, but Blackburn had ridden behind them, keeping to himself in more ways than one.

"Quiet one, ain't he?" McConnell asked.

Even while blowing the horses Blackburn chose to stand off on his own.

"What do you know about him?" Pike asked.

"How would I know anything about him?"

"You're bedding down with the camp gossip, aren't you?" Pike asked.

"Well . . . I wouldn't exactly call her the camp gossip," McConnell said.

"What would you call her?"

McConnell paused a moment, and then said, "Well-informed."

"Well, how well-informed is she about Blackburn?" Pike asked.

"Well . . . for one thing, she thinks he's in love with Rita."

"Oh that's just great," Pike said, moving his shoulders uncomfortably, "and he's been riding behind me all morning. That's fine."

"Don't worry," McConnell said, "I've been watchin' him good."

"You have."

"Sure," McConnell said, "the minute he put a ball in your back I would have put one in him."

"That's comforting."

They both turned then and looked at Blackburn, who was watching them with no expression on his face.

"He's got the blackest beard I ever seen," McConnell said.

"I was thinking the same thing."

"You haven't noticed anybody on our trail, have you?" McConnell asked, turning serious.

"No," Pike said, "but I've got the feeling we're being watched."

He'd had that feeling for the past hour, but hadn't mentioned it. He was waiting for McConnell to say something. If his friend felt the same way he did, then he was sure that they *were* being watched.

"If we're bein' watched," McConnell said, "and we can't see 'em, they must be Indians."

"Right."

"Think he knows?" McConnell asked, indicating Blackburn with a jerk of his head.

"I don't know," Pike said. "Why don't we find out."

They both left their horses and walked over to where Blackburn was standing.

"We're bein' watched," the man said, immediately. "I

can feel it."

"Right," Pike said, exchanging a glance with McConnell. "We figure Indians."

"Probably Crow."

"We ran into a Crow hunting party just before we arrived," McConnell said. "It could still be them hanging around."

"We'd better keep our guard up," Blackburn said.

"Good advice."

"You fellas didn't think I knew, did you?" Blackburn asked.

"We didn't know," Pike said.

"Well, now you do."

Pike nodded and said, "We'll be moving out in ten minutes."

"Fine. I'll be ready."

Pike and McConnell returned to their horses.

"Okay," Pike said, "he's got sharp eyes, and he's in love with Rita. What else do we know about him?"

"Well," McConnell said, "he doesn't like you."

Pike pinned his friend with a hard stare and said, "What else?"

"According to Sheila," McConnell said, "he's arrogant, but he's usually been able to back it up."

"Can he shoot?"

McConnell shrugged.

"That I can't say."

"Well," Pike said, "if we're all right about who's following us, we may find out pretty soon." Pike turned, signaled to Blackburn, and then said to McConnell, "Let's get moving."

*****

Small Bear watched the three white men mount up and start off on their horses again. He turned then and rode back to where Standing Wolf was waiting with the other Crow braves. There were a dozen in the hunting party, easily enough to handle three white men.

"They are moving again," Small Bear said to his leader, Standing Wolf.

"We will follow," Standing Wolf said.

"When do we attack?" Small Bear asked.

Standing Wolf gave Small Bear a withering look and said, "When I say it is time."

Small Bear, known for his impatience more than anything else, made a face and subsided.

"We go," Standing Wolf said.

When Cal Devers saw Pike, McConnell, and the black-bearded man—he had the *blackest* beard Devers had ever seen—ride out of camp he was tempted to follow them. He decided against it, because the skins were still in camp, and there were more to come. More than likely, Pike and the others were going to Fort Pierre to arrange for some mackinaws. Devers mentally patted himself on the back for that deduction. Fort Pierre was the closest location, and there was a boatyard nearby.

If only Pike and the others knew how predictable they were being. Well, they weren't being *that* predictable, Devers told himself. He was just outthinking them.

Just like he was outthinking them when he decided to stay behind and not follow Pike. More likely than not, Pike, McConnell, and the other man would be dealt with by a Crow or Snake hunting party. That would suit Devers fine, because then he wouldn't have to worry about dealing with Pike—and despite what he told his partner, LeConte, he *was* worried about the big man. Pike had a reputation in the mountains that couldn't be denied, but Devers wasn't about to give up a cache this big just because of one man.

Yeah, maybe the Indians would take that problem right out of his hands.

They stopped a half hour before dark and camped. Blackburn saw to the horses while McConnell scouted up the makings of a campfire. Pike kept an eye out, in case the Indian or Indians who were trailing them decided to come down for a visit.

Soon, they had a fire going, and a pot of coffee on it. The three of them sat around the fire as the temperature dropped due to the absence of the sun, and had coffee.

"We'll turn in early and set up three-hour watches," Pike said.

"I'll take the first watch," Blackburn said, and when both Pike and McConnell looked at him he added, "If no one minds?"

"No, go ahead," Pike said, waving a hand in a magnanimous gesture.

"What do you suppose they're waitin' for?" McConnell said.

"Well," Pike said, "they're either waiting for help, or they know that we know, and are leaving us to think about it for a while."

"Make us nervous," Blackburn said.

41

"Right."

"Well," he said, "that's not gonna work with me."

"Good," Pike said, "glad to hear it."

"I don't think they're waiting for help," McConnell said. "I mean, even if it's only one Crow brave out there, they have a tendency to believe that they're worth any three white men."

"They are worth almost any three white men I know," Blackburn said.

"Maybe so," McConnell said, glaring at Blackburn, "but not these three."

"We'd better turn in," Pike said to McConnell, trying to head off an argument. "Blackburn, wake me up for the second watch."

Blackburn nodded.

Pike and McConnell set up their bedrolls on the opposite side of the fire from Blackburn.

"What was that all about?" Pike whispered to McConnell.

"Why did he have to make that crack?"

"Maybe he believes it," Pike said. "You're supposed to be making sure that he and I don't get into it, and *you're* starting an argument with him."

"I didn't start it," McConnell said, "he did."

"Go to sleep, Skins," Pike said, wrapping himself up in his own blanket.

At first, he was lying with his back to the fire, and to Blackburn. On second thought, he turned around and faced Blackburn, and only then did he close his eyes.

The night went by without incident. Blackburn woke Pike without saying a word, and then turned in. Pike took up his position at the fire and poured himself a cup of coffee. He made another pot before waking McConnell.

"Sleeping Beauty over there say anything when he relieved you?" McConnell asked.

"He grunted," Pike said. He sat and had a cup of coffee with McConnell. The middle watch was always the hardest. The others got to sleep for five or six hours at a stretch. When you had the middle watch you slept three, watched for three, and then tried to sleep again. It wasn't always easy to get back to sleep.

"We've been through this before," McConnell said. "Why don't one of us double back and see what's happening?"

"We've doubled back on one or two men before," Pike said, "but we don't know how many are back there—if any. Maybe we're just imagining things."

"Not if we all feel it," McConnell said. "No, they're out there; I just don't know what they're waiting for."

"If they're going to come after us, they'll have to do it before we reach Fort Pierre." Pike dumped the remnants of his coffee into the fire, which flared briefly. "I'm going to try and get some more sleep. Wake us early so we can get an early start. I want to try and make Fort Pierre by nightfall."

"Right."

Pike turned in and left McConnell on watch.

McConnell stayed alert and when first light was at hand he woke Pike and Blackburn by touching them in turn.

"What?" Blackburn said.

"Morning," McConnell said, "time to get going."

"Is there any coffee?"

"Forget the coffee," Pike said, standing up and rolling his blanket. "Let's get started. I want to travel with more speed today."

"That might force them into making a move," McConnell said.

"I hope they do," Pike said, "I'm tired of waiting for them."

"No coffee?"

"You can have your coffee at lunchtime," McConnell said.

"No lunch," Pike said. "We're going to ride straight through."

"Now wait a minute—" Blackburn started.

"You wait a minute," Pike said. "Nobody invited you along, you invited yourself. If you want to stop for coffee, that's up to you. Skins and I are riding through until we reach Fort Pierre."

Pike walked away and heard McConnell following him. They started to saddle their horses. When he looked over at Blackburn the man was dousing the fire and kicking it apart to make sure it was dead.

Small Bear and Standing Wolf both looked down at the camp.

"They know we are here," Standing Wolf said.

"How would they know that?"

"Do you not recognize the tall one, Small Bear?" Standing Wolf asked.

Small Bear looked down at the three men and didn't dare admit that he did not.

"Of course."

"It is the one who is called He-Whose-Head-Touches-The-Sky. It is not possible that he does not know we are following. What he does not know is when we will attack."

"Then we should kill them now."

"We are too far. If we ride down on them now they will have time to react," Standing Wolf said.

"Then when?" Small Bear asked.

"We will close the distance, and attack them without giving them time to react," Standing Wolf said.

For Small Bear's taste, Standing Wolf was too careful a leader—but he *was* the leader.

"They are preparing to leave, and they look like they are in a hurry," Small Bear said.

"Then we are in a hurry, also," Standing Wolf said.

He turned and walked back to his horse as if he weren't in a hurry at all. Small Bear turned and followed, impatiently.

CHAPTER FIVE

"Wait."

McConnell and Blackburn both pulled up and looked at Pike.

"What is it, Pike?" McConnell said.

"I hear something."

They both listened.

"I don't hear anything," Blackburn said.

"Horses," McConnell said.

They turned and looked behind them and saw a band of Indians riding for them, hard.

"Here they come!" Pike yelled.

They dug into their horses and started off on the run. Pike's horse reacted more quickly and he was out in front two jumps. He didn't bother looking behind him to see if McConnell and Blackburn were behind him. If they weren't, there wasn't much he'd be able to do about it.

Riding a horse in the mountains is a chancy business at best. Riding one at top speed while being chased is even worse. One misstep and the horse would be down and useless. The man on his back would be as good as dead. They couldn't keep this pace up much longer. The best thing to do was find a place to hole up and hope that these particular Indians didn't have rifles. The three of them, with their firearms, could hold off a dozen or so Indians indefinitely—or until their powder ran out.

Or until more Indians came.

Pike chanced a look behind him now and saw McConnell right on his tail. Blackburn was off to the right and slightly behind McConnell, and Pike couldn't see him. McConnell saw him looking back and waved for him to turn around. He was probably thinking that Pike was going to ride into a tree.

Pike held his rifle up over his head and then pointed ahead with it. He hoped that McConnell would get the message. He also hoped that Blackburn would follow their lead.

He turned his eyes forward again, before he *did* ride into a tree, and started searching for some cover. After another hundred yards he saw a rock formation that looked promising. The problem was he'd have to commit to it, and wouldn't know if it *wasn't* promising until they dismounted to run to it.

Ah, what the hell. Somebody had to make a move.

John Blackburn wanted to turn and fight. After all, they were just Indians and they probably didn't have firearms. The problem was, he was riding behind Pike and McConnell, and if he stopped to fight, they wouldn't see him—and he wasn't about to stand and fight them by himself, guns or no guns.

48

He shouted out to McConnell, who was the closest to him, but the man either didn't hear him, or didn't want to hear him. He was about to shout again when suddenly Pike's horse swerved and Pike leaped from its back. The big man landed running, almost lost his balance and went down, then righted himself, pointed his rifle, and fired.

McConnell swerved his horse also, and Blackburn realized that he was getting his wish, to stop and fight—but was that what he really wanted?

He was about to find out.

Pike almost lost his balance when he landed, and he felt a pain in his knee as he twisted. He had no time to pay any attention to it, though. He raised his rifle and fired, and an Indian—possibly a Crow—fell from his saddle.

He drew his Kentucky pistol from his belt and started backing toward the rock formation he had chosen.

McConnell dropped from his horse and fell on his face. He recovered quickly, though, got to his knees, pointed his rifle and fired it. Another Indian was taken from his horse.

By this time Blackburn had leaped from his horse and was rolling on the ground. McConnell got to his feet as Pike fired his Kentucky pistol. He caught an Indian in the shoulder, but the brave stayed astride his horse.

McConnell grabbed Blackburn by the collar and dragged him to his feet. Pike made for the rocks, with McConnell and Blackburn behind him. By the time they got there Pike was reloading.

"Reload!" he shouted.

McConnell proceeded to do so, while Blackburn shouted, "I didn't fire, yet."

"Well, why the hell not?" Pike demanded.

"McConnell grabbed me before I had time to."

Pike, reloaded, stuck his head up to see where the Indians were.

They were nowhere in sight, except for two dead ones on the ground.

"They're gone," he said.

McConnell looked up and said, "Haven't gone far, I'd wager."

"How many guns you got, Blackburn?" Pike asked.

"Just the one."

"That gives us four between us," Pike said, counting his own Kentucky pistol. "They aren't going to charge four guns. Not when we've already taken a bite out of them."

"What *are* they gonna do, then?" Blackburn asked.

"Probably try to work some of them around behind us," McConnell said. "Pike, did you see any rifles on their side?"

"Not a one."

"Bows and arrows, then, and some lances."

"And our horses are gone," Blackburn said. "This was a real good idea, Pike." He had conveniently forgotten his own desire to stop and fight.

"Better than riding our horses until they dropped, or broke a leg."

"So what do we do now?"

Pike turned and sat with his back to the rock.

"We wait," he said, and McConnell sat down next to

him. "You keep watch, Blackburn. Let us know when you see an Indian."

"And don't fire as soon as you see one," McConnell said. "We're gonna have to make every shot count."

"I always make my shots count."

"When you make them," Pike added.

"What's that—"

"Never mind," McConnell said, cutting off an argument. "We got enough trouble right now without fighting among ourselves."

Grudgingly, Blackburn fell silent and watched.

"The horses can't be far," McConnell said. "Ours, anyway. I can probably round them up on foot."

"Too risky."

"Better to do it now than wait until some of them have worked their way behind us."

Pike thought a moment, then said, "All right. I'll cover you."

They both stood up and McConnell moved out from behind the rocks. There was no reaction from the Indians, who were sure to be within view.

"Here," Pike said, handing McConnell his Kentucky pistol. "Take this and leave your rifle."

"Right." McConnell tucked the pistol into his belt.

"Go!" Pike said, and McConnell started on the run after the horses.

"Here they come," Blackburn said.

Pike turned and laid his rifle barrel atop the rock.

"Wait," he said. "Let them get closer."

"How many men did we lose?" Standing Wolf asked.

"Two," Small Bear said, "and we have one injury."

"It was Pike," Standing Wolf said, using Pike's proper name for the first time. "The man has eyes like a hawk, and a steady hand."

"You admire him."

"Yes," Standing Wolf said, "don't you?"

"I *hate* him."

"Have a brave watch for movement. I want to know as soon as he sees something."

"All right."

Standing Wolf went to check on the injured brave, who insisted that he would be able to ride.

"Ride, yes," Standing Wolf said, laying his hand on the man's uninjured shoulder, "but you cannot use your bow. You will stay behind when we charge."

The brave reluctantly agreed.

"Standing Wolf," Small Bear said, "something is happening."

Standing Wolf turned in time to see one of the men dart from behind the rocks.

"He is going for the horses," Standing Wolf said. "Now we will charge."

"Yes!" Small Bear said triumphantly, and mounted up.

McConnell caught up with his and Pike's horse about twenty-five yards along. There was no sign of Blackburn's animal. He and Pike would have to find it later.

"Easy, boys," he said, approaching the horses. He had a hold of them when he heard the shots from behind him. He released Pike's horse, mounted his own, and started to ride back.

As the Indians charged them Pike could sense the tension in Blackburn.

"Now show me how you make your shots count," Pike said. "On my mark."

Pike waited . . . and waited . . . and waited. . . .

"Now!"

They both fired, and both shots were true. Two more braves fell from their horses. Blackburn started to reload while Pike raised McConnell's rifle. He fired, wounding a brave who did not fall.

"They're still coming!" he shouted as the Indians continued to come closer.

There were more than six when they reached the rocks and threw themselves at the two white men.

Pike stood up, reversed his rifle, and swung it. He struck a brave right in the chest, taking him from his horse. At the same time two braves landed on him, bearing him to the ground.

Blackburn had reloaded but as he stood to point his rifle two Indians collided with him, taking him to the ground. The rifle discharged, and the ball struck the already wounded brave. The unlucky man died instantly, this time.

Now it was to be hand-to-hand, Pike and Blackburn against six braves.

CHAPTER SIX

As Pike hit the ground with two Indians atop him he released his hold on his rifle and grabbed for his knife. For some reason both Indians seemed to be intent on pinning his right hand. They were working individually rather than as a team, and that left his left hand free. He drew the knife and thrust it into the side of one of the braves. He heard the man cry out in pain and go limp. As the brave died his dead weight fell on the other Indian, confusing him. He released Pike's arm and rolled away. Pike rolled the opposite way and came up with his knife ready. The Indian saw the blood on the knife and realized what had happened. He drew his own knife, and he and Pike stared at each other for a few moments before rushing each other.

As John Blackburn hit the ground he managed to grab one of the Indians atop him by the hair with his right hand. He pulled with all his strength and the brave had no choice but to go with it, or have his hair pulled out by the roots.

As the first Indian rolled off of Blackburn he balled

up his fist and struck the other a telling blow behind the head. That brave, his head buzzing, rolled off of him and Blackburn quickly got to his feet.

The Indian whose hair he had pulled had also gained his feet and now rushed the black-bearded white man. Blackburn nimbly sidestepped and used both hands to propel the Indian past him right into a boulder. The Indian struck headfirst with a wet sound, and slid to the ground.

Blackburn turned to the second Indian, who was halfway to his feet. He stepped into the man and drove a kick into the ribs. All the air left the brave's lungs and he made gagging sounds as he staggered about. Blackburn moved closer and struck the man a good, clean blow with his fist. The Indian slumped to the ground, unconscious.

Blackburn looked behind him and saw that Pike had dispatched one Indian and was facing another, both holding their knives. He decided that Pike could handle the brave himself.

He turned to look forward and saw that two Indians had not yet dismounted—and one of them was aiming a bow and arrow at him!

Standing Wolf decided not to dismount. He wanted to watch his four braves battle the two white men hand-to-hand. Both white men were big, Pike just a little larger than the younger, black-bearded man. Standing Wolf watched the fight with pleasure.

Small Bear had not dismounted because he had no desire to engage in hand-to-hand combat. He preferred to stay astride his horse and send an arrow into one of the white men. As he started to draw back on the bow, Standing Wolf stopped him with a single word.

"No."

Small Bear looked at his leader. The look on his face made it plain that he was not happy.

"Why not?"

"Let them fight," Standing Wolf said.

They watched the four men fight, and it soon became evident that the two white men would conquer the four Crow braves.

"Now?" Small Bear asked as the black-bearded man struck the second brave unconscious.

Standing Bear frowned, his eyes on Pike and the last brave, and said, "Yes."

With a gleam in his eye Small Bear once again pointed his bow at the white man with the black beard. In fact, it was the blackest beard Small Bear had ever seen.

At that moment the white man turned and looked into Small Bear's eyes.

Small Bear smiled triumphantly.

As McConnell came riding back into view he saw an Indian brave on a horse pointing his bow. He didn't know if the bow was pointed at Pike or Blackburn, but that didn't much matter. He quickly raised his rifle, pointed it rather than aimed it, and fired. As the ball struck the brave, he released the bowstring.

Blackburn watched as the Indian fell from his horse. The arrow had gone by his ear, and he imagined that it had even touched him.

The last Indian, still astride his horse, realized that he was now outnumbered three to one. He turned his horse and rode off. Blackburn wished his rifle were loaded so he could fire at him.

He turned to see who had saved his life, and saw McConnell riding toward him. He then turned around and saw Pike. He had grabbed hold of the brave's knife hand by the wrist, and now drove his own blade into the Indian's belly. After it had penetrated, Pike twisted the knife, then withdrew it. He stepped back so that the brave could fall forward.

Blackburn heard a groan from the Indian he had knocked unconscious. He turned and saw the man stirring. He took out his knife, straddled the man, grabbed him by the hair, pulled his head back so that his neck was exposed, and then drew the razor-sharp blade of his knife across the man's throat, opening it and spilling his blood all over the ground.

When he let the man's head fall to the ground, where it landed in the puddle of blood, he looked up and found McConnell staring down at him.

"That wasn't necessary," McConnell said.

Blackburn leaned down and drove his blade into the ground several times to clean the blood off.

"I think it was."

McConnell shook his head and looked over at Pike, who had not seen what Blackburn had done. Pike was cleaning his own knife. That done, he walked over to them.

"One of them got away," McConnell said. "I think he was the leader."

"He's bound to feel disgraced," Pike said. "I don't

58

think we need to fear anything from him anymore. I see you found the horses."

"Mine," McConnell said, "and yours is further on."

"What about mine?" Blackburn asked.

"I didn't see yours," McConnell said. "We'll have to look for it."

"I can ride double with one of you, then."

"Not with me," Pike said.

"Or me," McConnell said.

"Hey!"

"Like I said before," Pike said, "you weren't invited. You can walk until we find your horse."

"And if we don't?"

"There are plenty of Indian ponies in the area," Pike said. "Don't worry. We'll get you a horse."

"I don't want any damn Indian pony!"

"It might be that, or walk," McConnell said. "It's up to you."

Blackburn grumbled, but what he said wasn't audible to either Pike or McConnell, and they didn't ask him to repeat it.

"By the way," McConnell said to Blackburn.

"What?"

"You're welcome."

"For what?"

"For saving your life."

"Oh, that," Blackburn said. "I don't think you had a choice."

"You're right, I didn't," McConnell said. "I couldn't see who that Indian was pointing his bow at, you or Pike."

"Would it have made a difference?" Blackburn asked, arrogantly.

"Up to five minutes ago," McConnell said, "my answer to that question would have been no."

They found Blackburn's horse about a half mile away. It was standing in a clearing, its head bowed, drinking water from a small waterhole. Blackburn walked over to it and started checking it for damage.

"I know why I wouldn't let him ride double with me," Pike said to McConnell. "What's your excuse?"

"You didn't see what he did back there."

"I thought he did pretty well for himself."

McConnell told Pike how Blackburn had slit the throat of the helpless brave.

"Even an Indian deserves more respect than that," Pike said. He reacted to the incident with distaste. "He's a good fighter, but there's something missing from that fella inside."

"I agree," McConnell said. "I think we should keep an eye on him. There's no telling what a fella like that could do."

"All right," Pike said, "all right. We'll keep an eye on him the rest of the way. Right now we'd better get moving. If there are any other Indians in the area, they must have heard the ruckus."

CHAPTER SEVEN

Fort Pierre was a fairly large settlement, probably the largest on the Missouri, which is why a boatyard had been built nearby.

It was dark when Pike, McConnell, and Blackburn rode in. They would have to put off going to the boatyard until morning. All they wanted now was a hot meal and a place to sleep.

"Blackburn," Pike said, "take the horses to be cared for."

"Hey," Blackburn said, "I'm hungry, too."

"We'll save you a seat," Pike said, dismounting and handing the man his reins. McConnell did the same thing.

"Well, order me a steak so I don't have to wait when I come back."

"Sure," Pike said.

"And some hot coffee."

"It won't be hot anymore by the time you get back."

"Right, right," Blackburn said. "I'll order my own coffee."

Pike and McConnell watched Blackburn ride away leading their horses, and then walked over to the trading post.

Pike hadn't been to Fort Pierre for a couple of years, but when he entered he was recognized immediately by Jim Hillerman, the big man standing behind the counter.

"Pike! What the hell are you doin' on the Missouri?" Hillerman asked.

Pike and McConnell approached the counter, and Pike shook Hillerman's hand. Hillerman was a big, barrel-chested man in his sixties, whose barrel chest had fallen some into his stomach. Both were covered now by a dirty white apron. He had short, gray hair and big ears, and a storytelling ability that held even the most straight-faced mountain man in rapt attention.

"Jim Hillerman, Skins McConnell."

Hillerman nodded to McConnell, and they shook hands.

"What brings you boys out so late?"

Pike looked around the place, which was empty. Anyone who was going to have dinner here had already had it.

"Can we get three steaks, Jim? I'll explain better after we've had some coffee, too."

"Three steaks and three coffees comin' right up," Hillerman said, rubbing his big, red, chapped hands together.

Pike didn't bother telling him just to bring out two coffees.

"Beer?" Hillerman asked.

"After dinner," Pike said.

"Sit yourselves down," Hillerman said. "I'll bring

the steaks out to you."

"Thanks, Jim."

Pike was used to sitting at makeshift tables made from boards or barrels. Here, Hillerman had hand built his own tables and chairs, and there were six to choose from. Pike and McConnell chose the one furthest from the front door.

Hillerman came out with three cups of steaming coffee and set them down on the table.

"The steaks are on, should be ready soon."

"Make 'em nice and red," McConnell said.

"That's the only way to eat 'em," Hillerman said. "You fellas got another friend with you?"

"Let's just say there's a third man with us and leave it at that."

Hillerman grinned and went back around behind the counter. He was bringing out the steaks when Blackburn came through the door.

The first thing Blackburn did when he sat down was take a sip of coffee.

"Ah, it's not hot," he complained.

Hillerman set the plates on the table and then picked up Blackburn's cup.

"I'll get you a hot cup. In fact, I'll bring a pot to the table."

Pike waited for Blackburn to say something, and when he didn't Pike said, "Thanks, Jim."

"Sure."

After Hillerman left, Pike leaned over and said to Blackburn, "Where did you learn your manners?"

Blackburn, his mouth full of red meat, stared across at Pike with a puzzled look on his face.

"He doesn't even know what I'm talking about,"

Pike said to McConnell.

"Forget it, Pike," McConnell said.

"What?" Blackburn said.

"Forget it," Pike said in disgust.

Hillerman returned with a pot of coffee and set it down on the table.

"So, what are you boys doin' around here?"

"We've been hunting downriver," Pike said, "and we're about ready to transport our goods. We came here to go to the boatyard and have them build us some mackinaws."

"Mackinaws!" Hillerman said, his eyes gleaming. "I ain't been on a mackinaw in years."

"That's right, you were pretty handy on a mackinaw in your day, weren't you?"

"In my day," Hillerman said, staring at Pike. "I could still handle one. You let me know if you need any help."

"We will, Jim."

"You boys enjoy your dinner."

Hillerman went back around behind his counter, leaving them to eat.

"Imagine that old geezer on a mackinaw?" Blackburn said.

"Hey," Pike said, "watch your mouth. He was working mackinaws while you were still sucking your mother's tit."

"You ain't really thinking about using him, are you?" Blackburn asked.

"Maybe we'll use him instead of you."

"You can't," Blackburn said. "I accounted for a lot of those skins and I'm seein' them downriver."

Pike and McConnell exchanged a glance. McConnell knew that Pike wasn't serious about using Jim Hillerman.

"Look," Pike said to both of them, "in the morning I'll go over to the boatyard and make the arrangements. There's no reason you two have to come along."

"I got nothing else to do," McConnell said.

"Me neither."

Pike shrugged and said, "Fine. We'll camp just outside of the settlement and walk over to the boatyard early."

"Do we know where it is?" McConnell said.

"It's got to be right on the river," Pike said. "I'll ask Jim on the way out."

"When do we start back?" Blackburn asked.

"As soon as we come to terms with the boatyard people," Pike said.

"We're gonna have to pay somethin' up front," McConnell said.

"I got some money from Harley for that," Pike said. "All we have to do is agree on a price."

"For two boats?" McConnell asked.

"Two," Pike said, nodding. "That should be enough."

Satisfied that they knew what they were going to do, they fell on their food and finished without another word.

When they were finished, McConnell and Blackburn went outside while Pike went to the counter to pay for their meals.

After he had paid he said, "Jim, where's the boatyard located?"

"Due west, Pike," Hillerman said. "Just keep walkin'

until you come to the river. You can't miss it."

"The boatyard or the river?" Pike asked with a grin.

Hillerman laughed and said, "Take your pick."

They pitched their beds in a clearing west of the settlement and turned in. They didn't feel any need to set a watch.

In the morning McConnell woke first and put on a pot of coffee. The smell woke Pike and Blackburn. They all had a cup, and then started walking to the boatyard.

The boatyard was literally on the river. There was a dock that extended right out onto the river, and there was a slip that had been dug out so that they could literally build boats on the river itself. As they approached they could hear the sounds of hammering and sawing. They apparently started work very early.

"Look at it," McConnell said, staring out at the Missouri. It was impressive, the current moving downstream fairly quickly, but during the June rise it would be moving even faster.

"Let's go," Pike said.

A high wooden fence had been built around the yard, with a gate. As they went through the gate they saw a wooden structure on the opposite side of the slip. Around them the sounds of hammering and sawing persisted, louder still.

They walked around the slip to the wooden structure that was little more than a shack.

"Hello, inside!" Pike called.

A man stepped into the doorway, wiping his hand off on a cloth.

"Hello yourself," the man said. "Can I help ya?"

He was in his forties, very tall but painfully thin. His hair was sandy and sparse, his chin long and pointed. The hands he was wiping were remarkably graceful-looking, with long, tapered fingers.

"My name is Pike," Pike said, making the introductions. "This is McConnell and Blackburn."

"Pleased to meetcha," the man said. "My name's Pebbles, Jamie Pebbles. What can I do for ya?"

Pike explained that they had been hunting downriver for a few months and, come the June rise, would like to take their goods downriver by mackinaw.

"Can you build us two?"

"Mackinaws, eh?" the man said. "Sure, I can build 'em better than anybody—for the right price."

Pike turned and looked at McConnell, who nudged Blackburn. They walked away to allow Pike to dicker with the man in private.

"Come on," McConnell said, walking toward the dock.

"Where?" Blackburn asked.

"I want to walk out on the dock."

Blackburn balked and said, "Out there?"

McConnell, who had already stepped out onto the dock, turned and looked at Blackburn.

"Come on!"

"Out there?" Blackburn asked again.

McConnell stepped down off the dock and faced Blackburn.

"You don't mean to tell me you're scared to walk out on the dock?"

"I'm not . . . scared. I just don't see any reason to . . . right now."

67

"Blackburn," McConnell said, setting his hands on his hips, "if you can't walk out on a dock, how do you intend to go downriver on a mackinaw?"

"I'll go, don't worry."

"I do worry," McConnell said. "We're gonna need men who aren't worried that they're gonna fall off. Now, come out on the dock with me."

"Whataya want to go out there for, anyway?"

"I want to get a close look at the river."

"I can see it well enough from here."

"Jesus—" McConnell said. "Why don't you just walk out there with me to prove you can do it?"

"I don't have to prove anythin' to you," Blackburn said.

"I wasn't talkin' about provin' it to me."

After Pike and Pebbles had agreed on a price Pike went looking for McConnell and Blackburn. He saw them out on the dock, walking back from the edge, and they looked odd. It looked as if Blackburn was holding onto McConnell's arm. Pike had the feeling that if McConnell had let go of the man, Blackburn would have fallen off.

Pike walked to the end of the dock to meet them.

"What's going on?" he asked.

"Nothing," McConnell said as he and Blackburn stepped off the dock. Pike noticed that Blackburn was sweating profusely even though it was a cool day. Also, the younger man would not meet Pike's eyes. The bravado, the youthful arrogance that was almost always in evidence was now totally absent.

"Did you settle on a price?" McConnell asked.

"Yep," Pike said, "but we have to supply the skins that they'll use for the roof of each mackinaw. We'll have to come back once again with them."

"Maybe we ought to bring more men next time," McConnell said, "just in case we run into another hunting party."

"Good idea."

Pike looked at Blackburn's back as the man walked away from the dock. He wasn't moving too steadily, as if he were still walking on the dock.

"What happened with him?"

"I think he's afraid of the water," McConnell said. "I almost had to drag him out onto the dock."

"If he's afraid of the water," Pike said, "he's not going to be much good on a mackinaw."

"He insists that he'll be all right."

"He'd better be," Pike said, again looking at the retreating man, "because nobody's going to hold his arm once we get on board."

"Well," McConnell said, "that's gonna be his problem, isn't it?"

"It sure is," Pike said, "because it sure as hell isn't going to be mine."

CHAPTER EIGHT

They started back for the camp that afternoon. Little was said about Blackburn's reaction to the walk on the dock. Pike would take up the matter with Harley Rose when they got back.

The trip back was uneventful. They set watches for the night, but there was no sign of any Indians at all. When they passed by the location of their short-lived battle, the bodies of the braves were still there. That surprised Pike and McConnell. The Indians usually picked up their dead. This meant that the one Indian who had escaped—probably the leader—had not wished to disgrace himself further by leading a recovery party back to the scene. He had probably told some great whopping lie to cover for himself. Pike didn't know who the brave was, but he was obviously without the honor that the Indians so prided themselves on.

When they arrived in camp they were greeted by Harley Rose and several other men. Sheila also came running out to greet McConnell. Rita was nowhere in sight.

Pike had a cup of coffee with Rose and laid it all out for him, everything that had happened, and the deal he had made at the boatyard.

"When will we have to bring the skins in?" Rose asked.

"A couple of weeks, at least," Pike said. "I'd like to take more men with me that time."

"No problem."

"I'd like to leave Blackburn behind."

"Why?"

Pike hesitated, then said, "Will you accept personal reasons as an answer?"

"I don't think so," Rose said. "See, I think a lot of Blackie. I think he's gonna make a crackerjack hunter, and in the future he might even be a fine booshway. If you know any reason why I'm wrong, I'd like to know about it."

Pike stared at Rose for a few moments, then shook his head and said, "No, no reason."

Cal Devers saw Pike, McConnell, and the other men return. Obviously, they had either not run into an Indian hunting party, or the Indians had been unable to do the job for him. Well, that was okay. When the time came, he'd do the job himself.

A couple of weeks later, when Pike, McConnell, and six men left camp, Henri LeConte was present, with four other men he had recruited.

"Henri," Devers called.

"*Oui?*"

72

"Follow them," Devers said. "See where they're goin'."

"Where do you think they are goin', *mon ami?*" LeConte asked.

"Probably to the boatyard at Fort Pierre," Devers said. "They're bringin' skins, which the boat builder would need for a mackinaw."

"Why don't I take the men and take the skins away from them?"

"Don't be stupid," Devers said. "What they've got there is a pittance compared to what we can take later. Besides, you'd be outnumbered. No, I just want you to follow them and make sure they've made their deal for the mackinaws."

"And if they have?"

"We'll have to start lookin' for a place along the river for us to make our move," Devers said. "Now get goin' before they get too much of a head start."

"Oui."

"And don't let them see you," Devers called after him. "Don't get careless."

Devers was feeling the anticipation inside. From his vantage point he could see that the flow of the Missouri had already picked up speed. It wouldn't do to ruin things now by getting careless.

"What are you doin' back here so soon?" Jim Hillerman asked Pike.

"Brought you some more business, Jim," Pike said.

Hillerman looked at the men who were filing in after Pike and said, "I can see that. Steaks?"

"Yep," Pike said, "steaks."

73

The men fanned out and sat at the table, but Pike remained at the counter to talk to Hillerman.

"Bringin' in the skins for the mackinaws?" Hillerman asked, handing Pike a cup of coffee.

"How'd you know that?"

"You're having Pebbles build mackinaws for you, right?" Hillerman said. "He'd make you supply the skins yourself. That's his style."

"Is he any good?"

Hillerman nodded and said, "Damned good. If he builds you a mackinaw, it ain't gonna fall apart on you—not under normal circumstances, that is."

"That's good to hear."

Once again they had arrived too late to talk to Pebbles immediately, so Pike would go over in the morning with the skins. This time, however, he'd bring only McConnell with him, and he got no argument from Blackburn.

In fact, Blackburn had been very quiet since their last visit to Fort Pierre. Maybe the man wouldn't protest when Pike tried to keep him off the mackinaw details.

McConnell came up next to Pike and told Hillerman, "I'll have my steak here with Pike, Jim."

"Right."

Hillerman walked around the counter to bring the other men their steaks first.

"We were followed, you know," McConnell said.

"You noticed?"

"Yep."

"A white man."

"That's what I think," McConnell said. "The question is, why?"

"Why would a white man follow us, and try not to

74

be seen?"

"Maybe he intended to rob us?"

"One man robbing six?" Pike said. "Not very likely."

"Then he's watching us."

"Why?"

"To see where we're goin'."

"Why?"

McConnell thought a moment, then said, "Maybe somebody's plannin' on robbin' us, and is keepin' track of our movements."

"Haven't you had the feeling at all over the last few weeks that the camp has been being watched?" Pike asked, thoughtfully.

McConnell gave Pike a quick look and said with a frown, "No, why, have you?"

McConnell was normally more observant than he had been since meeting Sheila. The blond woman must have really turned his head.

"From time to time," Pike said. "I thought it was Indians, but maybe it wasn't."

"You think someone *is* plannin' to rob us?"

"Maybe."

"That's crazy," McConnell said. "There's too many of us. Why, we've got over forty men in camp, and some women who can shoot, too."

"I know," Pike said as Hillerman set a plate in front of each of them, "but what if they're not planning to hit us in camp?"

"You mean, on the trail? We'd still be a strong force—"

"I mean," Pike said, "on the river. We'll only be twelve on the river, Skins."

"How can they rob us on the river?"

"That's the question, all right," Pike said, cutting into his steak. "How?"

They all left Hillerman's at the same time, but Pike touched McConnell's arm to hold him back.

"If we were followed," he said, "then whoever it was might get hungry, or thirsty."

"You want me to stay here and watch the place, see if any other strangers come in?"

"Yes."

McConnell made a face and then gave his shoulders a resigned shrug.

"How long?"

"As long as you think necessary," Pike said. "If no one shows up in the next hour, I'd quit if I was you."

"Right."

"Walk with me now, just in case he's watching, and then double back and watch from hiding."

"Hiding?"

"Stand behind a tree, or something."

"Right," McConnell said, "a tree."

"Come on, come on," Pike said, "stop complaining."

"I'm not complaining," McConnell said. "I'm just wondering why I get all the good jobs."

Henri LeConte watched as the men from the camp left the trading post. The big man, Pike, and his friend McConnell were the last to leave. LeConte's stomach was rumbling, and he wanted a drink, but he dared not go in while the others were there. Now that they were gone, though, it was a different story.

He left his vantage point behind a tree and started for the trading post.

From *his* vantage point behind a tree, after doubling back, McConnell watched a man enter the trading post. Whether or not the man was a stranger to the settlement he didn't know. He'd have to find that out from Pike's friend Jim Hillerman.

LeConte entered the trading post and looked around carefully. Satisfied that the place was empty but for the proprietor, he approached the counter.

"Help ya?" Jim Hillerman asked.

"I would like somethin' to eat," LeConte said, "And to drink?"

"Sure," Hillerman said. "Steak do ya?"

"Oui—I mean, yes, thank you. A steak would be fine. Do you have beer?"

"Sure do," Hillerman said. "Huntin' hereabouts, or just travelin' through?"

"I would like zat steak as soon as possible," LeConte said.

"Sure, friend," Hillerman said. "Just tryin' to be friendly. Have a seat and I'll get that steak for ya."

McConnell went around behind the settlement to the back door, which was unlocked. He entered and found himself in a storeroom. He walked to a curtained doorway, looked out and saw Jim Hillerman standing at a stove preparing a steak. There were hunks of fresh

77

meat hanging from the ceiling, which led McConnell to believe that Jim Hillerman did his own hunting, and daily.

"Jim."

Hillerman started and looked over at McConnell.

"What are you doin' sneakin' around back here?" he asked.

"The fella you're makin' that steak for," McConnell said. "Do you know him?"

"Never saw him before."

"Who is he?"

"Don't know," Hillerman said. "All I know is he's a Frenchie."

"Talk to him," McConnell said, "see what you can find out."

"What's the matter?"

"Pike thinks someone may have been following us," McConnell said, "and this might be the man."

"All right," Hillerman said, sliding the steak from the frying pan into a plate, "He's not real talkative, but I'll see what I can find out from him. Are you gonna be back here?"

"We'll come back in the mornin' and talk to you," McConnell said. "I don't think this fella's gonna go anywhere tonight."

Hillerman nodded, and went out to bring the Frenchman his steak.

McConnell, his eyes heavy-lidded, left by the back door and went to turn in.

McConnell found Pike and the others bedded down outside of the settlement, where he, Pike, and Black-

78

burn had camped the last time they were there. As he rolled himself into his blanket, Pike stirred.

"Well?"

"Well what?" McConnell said, sleepily. "You were right. A stranger showed up after we left."

"Who is he?"

"I don't know," McConnell said. "Your friend Hillerman is feedin' him, and findin' out what he can. We can check back with him in the mornin'."

McConnell turned over and went to sleep. Pike decided that was all he was going to get from his friend, and also rolled over and went back to sleep.

CHAPTER NINE

In the morning Pike took a couple of men with him to deliver the skins to the boatyard. McConnell went alone to the trading post to talk to Jim Hillerman.

Pebbles had some men help Pike's men unload the skins, and then took Pike to see how far the mackinaws had progressed. Although they were basically skeletons, both boats looked to be extremely strongly built. One was out at the edge of the dock, and one was situated in the slip and was presently being worked on.

"Another couple of weeks and they should be ready," Pebbles said.

Pike was impressed with both the quality of the workmanship and the speed with which the work was progressing, and he said so.

"You won't find a finer mackinaw anywhere. What do you intend to do with them after you've finished with them?" Pebbles asked.

Pike hesitated to tell him that they would probably

sell the boats for firewood, but finally did.

Pebbles shook his head sadly and said, "It's a shame you couldn't get them back upriver. I hate to think of them being broken up."

"There isn't much else we can do with them, Mr. Pebbles," Pike said, apologetically.

"I know that," Pebbles said. "It's still a damned shame."

Pike told Pebbles that they would return in two weeks to take the boats off his hands.

"Can we load here?" he asked.

"Sure," Pebbles said. "I'll have both boats tied to the end of the dock."

"Fine," Pike said. "Thanks very much."

After offloading the skins Pike told the other men to go and get some breakfast, so Pike left the boatyard alone, with intentions of meeting up with McConnell at Jim Hillerman's trading post.

When McConnell reached the trading post it was doing a brisk business despite the early hour. He waited at one end of the counter until Hillerman had served all of his customers.

"You're early," Hillerman said. "Do you want breakfast?"

"Just coffee," McConnell said, "and information."

"I got the coffee," Hillerman said, "but not much in the way of information."

"I'll take what I can get."

Hillerman went to get the coffee while McConnell waited at the end of the counter.

Henri LeConte had awakened early and had taken

up a vantage point far enough away from the boatyard so that he could see but not be seen. He watched Pike and his men bring the skins into the boatyard on mules, and the men came out with empty mules. Pike remained inside for a short time, and then also came out. LeConte could see one mackinaw at the end of the dock. He had no way of knowing if there were more, but Cal Devers seemed to think that two such boats would be enough.

LeConte had a decision to make now. He had verified that Pike had come to Fort Pierre to have mackinaws built. That was what Devers wanted. Should he return now to their position above Pike's camp, or should he wait until Pike left and follow him back. Devers's instructions were to follow Pike and the others, so he decided that was what he would do. Until then, he was going to have to stay out of sight.

"All I got was his first name," Hillerman said. "Henri—only he pronounced it different—you know, with his Frenchie accent."

"He didn't say why he was here?"

"Like I said last night," Hillerman said, "he wasn't real talkative."

"A lot of people aren't talkative," McConnell said.

"Well, he seemed to be real . . . anxious not to say anythin' about himself."

"Uh-huh," McConnell said, sipping his coffee.

Before he could go on, the door opened and Blackburn and the other men came walking in.

"Looks like a breakfast rush," McConnell said. "I better get my order in now."

Donna Lee saw the big man walking toward the trading post and knew instinctively that he was Pike. She had heard several weeks ago that he had put in an order at the boatyard for two mackinaws. Obviously, he and his people were going to be taking some skins and goods downriver—and she wanted to go with them.

Donna was thirty, and had been at the Fort Pierre settlement for the past ten years. She had been stranded there when the man she had arrived with—an older man—died of a heart attack. She had watched Fort Pierre grow slowly, and although it was much more than it had been ten years ago, it wasn't enough for her now.

She had to get out, and Pike seemed her best bet.

Pike noticed the woman as he approached the trading post. She was medium height and in her shirt and jeans she appeared well-built along strong lines. Her hair was cut short, and was dark brown. She seemed to be moving to intercept him. Sure enough, as he got closer to the post, she moved into his path and waited with her hands on her hips.

"Are you Pike?" she asked. She was squinting, as the sun was to his back and she was looking up at him.

"That's right. What can I do for you?"

"I'll tell you what you can do for me, Mr. Pike," the woman said.

"Just Pike."

"You can take me downriver with you."

84

"What?"

"You're goin' downriver with some skins, aren't you? I mean, you are having some mackinaws built?"

"Well, yeah, but—"

"I need a ride."

"Miss—"

"Lee, Donna Lee."

"Miss Lee, I'm only taking six men per boat, and all six men are going to have to work very hard."

"Are your twelve men all experienced on mackinaws?" she asked.

"Well, no, but—"

"I am."

He looked at her in surprise.

"You've worked on mackinaws?"

"Several times," she said, "and you're gonna need at least a couple of experienced hands on each boat."

Pike took a moment to examine her. She was about thirty, no kid by any means, and she certainly appeared sturdy enough to work on a mackinaw.

"And you wouldn't want any payment for this?"

"Just passage," she said.

"To where?"

"Anywhere. St. Joe, St. Louis, wherever you drop your goods you can drop me." She seemed to sense that he was thinking about it. "What do you say?"

"I'd have to talk to some people about it," he said. "I'm not making these decisions myself."

"You're in charge, though, aren't you?"

"I'm not booshway, if that's what you mean."

"No," she said, "what I mean is, you're Jack Pike."

"Well, that means more to some people than others," he said. "I'll have to let you know. You'll be here in a couple of weeks?"

"I been here for years, I'll be here another couple of weeks for sure," she said, "but you ain't meanin' to bring your goods here, are you?"

"How else would we load them on the boats?" he asked.

"That's easy," she said. "Take the boats downriver and stop near your camp. You can load there. Carrying your goods from your camp to here is unnecessary travel time."

He stared at her because what she said made so much sense that he felt embarrassed for not having thought of it himself.

"Miss Lee—"

"Donna."

"Donna . . . I think you just bought yourself passage."

When Pike entered the trading post McConnell, Blackburn, and the others were engrossed in their breakfasts.

McConnell was eating alone at the counter and Pike joined him, staring hungrily at the eggs and potatoes his friend was eating.

"Yours is on the stove," Hillerman said from behind the counter. Pike looked up and the older man handed him a cup of coffee.

"Thanks, Jim."

"All set?" McConnell asked.

"Yep. What about you?"

"Fella following us is a Frenchie named Henri."

Pike waited a moment, then said, "And?"

86

"And nothin'. That's all Hillerman was able to get from him. He was real closemouthed about who he was and where he was goin'."

"Henri," Pike repeated. "Not exactly an unusual French name."

McConnell shrugged and said, "Chances are he'll follow us back to camp. Maybe we can make his acquaintance somewhere along the way."

"That might not be a bad idea," Pike said. "By the way, we've picked up a passenger."

"For what?"

"To work one of the boats," Pike said. "She'll be coming back to camp with us."

"She?" McConnell said, surprised. "We're takin' a woman on one of the mackinaws?"

"She'll earn her keep," Pike said. "In fact, she already has . . ." He went on to tell McConnell about Donna Lee, and her suggestion for loading the boats downriver instead of lugging the skins to Fort Pierre.

"Makes sense," McConnell said. "How come we didn't think of it?"

"I don't know."

"You talkin' about Donna Lee?" Hillerman asked, putting a plate of eggs and potatoes in front of Pike.

"That's right. You know her?"

"Everyone here does. Came here about ten years ago with an old trapper who was keepin' her. He dropped dead, and she's been here ever since."

"What'd she do?" McConnell asked. "Love him to death?"

"That's what I understand," Hillerman said.

McConnell looked at him and said, "I was kiddin'."

"I ain't," he said. "The way I hear it, they was in their

tent together, doin' what men and women do, and he up and died."

"Sounds like a dangerous woman."

"'Course," Hillerman added, "she weren't more'n twenty, and he was sixty, so that might have had somethin' to do with it."

"I would say," McConnell said. He looked at Pike and asked, "Where is she?"

"She's gettin' her horse. She'll meet us out front after we break camp."

"And when is that gonna be?" McConnell asked.

Around a mouthful of eggs Pike said, "As soon as I finish these eggs."

After breakfast they walked to camp and collected their horses and mules. John Blackburn had said very little during the trip, and during the stay. Pike was deciding that he liked the man better that way. However, when he told the men that they would be bringing a woman back to camp with them, and that she'd be working one of the mackinaws, Blackburn had something to say.

"What right does she have to work one of the boats?" he asked. "She ain't even part of our camp."

"We need experienced hands, Blackburn," Pike said, "and we don't have that many. She doesn't want any payment, just passage."

Blackburn looked around at the other men, looking for some support.

"Harley's gonna hear about this," he said lamely, when none was forthcoming.

"I know he is," Pike said, "because I'm going to tell

him about it when we get back. If he votes against it, then she's out. I told her that and she understands it."

"Well . . ." Blackburn said, trying to salvage some face, "she better."

"Let's go," Pike said, mounting up. "She'll be waiting for us in front of the trading post."

When they reached the trading post Donna Lee was sitting a gray horse, waiting in front.

"Ready?" Pike asked.

"I'm ready," she said.

"This is Skins McConnell," he said. She nodded and Skins said hello. "The others you can meet on the way."

"That's okay," she said. "I didn't sign on to make any new friends."

Blackburn made a sound and Pike said to Donna Lee, "Good, because you got a head start there."

CHAPTER TEN

The trip back to camp was once again uneventful. A stranger riding into camp with them attracted some attention.

"Found a friend?" Harley Rose asked as Pike dismounted and handed his reins to someone.

"Her name is Donna Lee," Pike said. "We have to talk about her. Do we have someplace for her to stow her gear?"

"Uh, sure, I guess so. I'll have Sheila take care of her, and then we can talk."

"Good. I'll meet you at your tent in twenty minutes," Pike said. "Oh, and don't talk to Blackburn before you talk to me."

Rose looked like he wanted to ask a question, but then he closed his mouth and nodded.

Pike went to his tent and found Rita there waiting for him.

His relationship with Rita had gotten complicated. She was holding on too tightly to him, and he didn't want her thinking that he would replace her husband.

"I see you brought a woman back with you," she said. "Is she yours?"

"We're going to use her to work one of the mackinaws," he said. "She's working for passage. That's it."

"Oh, really? You probably wanted to leave me, but you can't, so this is the way you're gonna get rid of me, by bringin' a woman back with you."

"Rita," Pike said, "when we're ready to take the skins downriver, that's when I'll be leaving. You knew that from the start."

"I thought—" she said, then cut herself off bitterly. "Oh, the hell with what I thought." She stormed past him to the tent flap, and then turned to face him. "Don't worry, Pike. You won't have to worry about me. I won't bother you anymore."

"Rita—" he said, but she walked out without another word.

He thought about going after her, but decided to leave well enough alone. If this was the break, then it was what he had been looking for. It didn't happen exactly the way he would have wanted, but it did happen.

He wanted to wash up before he went to talk to Rose, so he stripped down and washed with water from a basin. He put on fresh clothes, and left the tent to talk to Rose about Donna Lee.

"Blackburn was by," Rose said.

"I thought he might be."

Pike and Rose were sitting outside of Rose's tent, each with a cup of coffee.

"He's all hot and bothered about something," Rose

92

said. "I think it's that gal you brought in with you."

"Let me tell you about her," Pike said, and did. Rose listened patiently. "What do you think?" Pike asked.

"Well, if you think she's gonna be of help, then I'll stand by your decision, Pike," Rose said.

"And Blackburn?"

"I'll explain it to him."

"There's another thing, Harley," Pike said. "I didn't mention this last time, but . . ."

"But what?"

"I don't think Blackburn is going to be much help on a mackinaw."

"A lot of us have never worked on a mackinaw before, Pike," Rose said. "As long as I been huntin' I never been on one."

"He's afraid of the water."

"What?"

"Blackburn. He's afraid of the water."

"What are you talkin' about?"

Pike told Rose about Blackburn's reaction to just walking out on the dock.

"I don't know how he's going to work on a mackinaw if he's constantly worried about falling in."

"Let me talk to him, Pike," Rose said. "To tell you the truth, I kind of figured he'd go along to represent me, sort of."

Pike thought that over a moment, then said, "Look, Harley, the least I can do is back you on this. Whatever you decide is all right with me. If you want Blackburn to go along, we'll figure something out."

"Thanks, Pike."

"Did you find a place for Donna to bed down?"

"Sure did," Rose said. "She's gonna share Sheila's

93

tent for a while."

Pike laughed.

"I'm sure McConnell won't be too happy to hear that," he said.

"He's not," Rose said. "But you said you wouldn't mind if he moved in with you."

Pike scratched his head and said, "I guess I deserve that. Sure, no problem. I've shared a tent with Skins enough times."

"What about Rita?"

"What about her?" Pike asked.

"Oh, it's like that, is it?"

"Look, Harley, Rita had to realize sooner or later that I wasn't going to replace her husband."

"I saw her a while ago," Rose said. "She looks like she's gone back to hatin' men."

"Me *and* her husband, in particular, I'm sure," Pike said. "Ah, I'm sorry this had to happen. She and I should never have gotten involved."

"Well, I guess that's my fault."

"It's nobody's fault," Pike said. "It just didn't work out."

"I guess."

Pike dumped the remnants of his cup into the fire and stood up.

"There's something else we discovered while we were at Fort Pierre."

"What's that?"

"We were followed."

"Indians?"

"No," Pike said, "a white man—a Frenchman."

"One man?"

"Yes."

Rose hesitated and then said, "An advance man?"

"Checking us out," Pike said. "That's what Skins and I think."

Both men resisted the impulse to look up at high ground. If they were being watched, that's where it would be from.

"Somebody's plannin' to hit us," Harley Rose said.

"Looks like."

"What did you find out about the man?"

"His name's Henri," Pike said, "and he's good. It took Skins and me to spot him, and on the way back we *knew* he was there, but we couldn't spot him."

"LeConte!" Rose said, triumphantly.

"What?"

"Henri LeConte," Rose said. "It's got to be him."

"LeConte," Pike said, shaking his head. "I don't know him."

"He runs with Cal Devers."

"Uh-huh," Pike said. "That name I know. Devers is a thief."

"He and LeConte have been working together for a while."

"It's been a while since I've run across Devers," Pike admitted, "and I'm not looking forward to it."

"Why not?"

Pike looked at Rose and said, "Because I'll probably kill him."

Devers listened intently to LeConte's report of Pike's movement in Fort Pierre.

"And did they spot you?" he asked when LeConte was finished.

"Mon ami," LeConte said, scolding his partner, "who can see me when I do not want to be seen?"

Devers didn't answer, but he thought to himself if anyone could spot the Frenchman it would be Jack Pike.

"All right," Devers said. "We have enough men now. While you were gone those four you hired last month finally found their way here."

He didn't actually mean "here." The men he and LeConte had hired—including some Indians—were camped a couple of miles further downriver, where there was no danger of them running into anyone from Pike's camp. Even if they did, they'd just see some men camped along the river.

"What we have to figure out now is, where are they gonna load the skins, here or in Fort Pierre?"

"They are probably going to do it at the boatyard," LeConte said.

"I don't think so."

"Why not?"

"They haven't got enough mules to transport them."

"They can get more mules."

"And if they do," Devers said, "that will be our tip-off."

"I think we should start talkin' to the men to see who's gonna be ridin' those mackinaws downriver," Pike said. "We'll have to work with them."

"I'll get them together tonight," Rose said, "after dinner."

"I figure we've got four spots covered with me, Skins, Blackburn, and Donna Lee," Pike explained. "We need eight more men. Once we've got them Skins and I will start working with them."

Pike told Rose about Donna's idea about loading the skins right here rather than dragging them to Fort Pierre.

"Sounds good," Rose said. "We wouldn't have to go out and get so many extra mules. How come we didn't think of that?"

"I've been wondering that myself," Pike admitted.

"What about Devers and LeConte?" Rose said. "Should we send some men out looking for them?"

"No," Pike said. "If they don't know that we know they're watching, we'll have an advantage."

"The two of them can't do it alone, Pike," Rose said. "They've got to have some men with them, and *they* have to be camped somewhere."

"Probably miles from here, up or downriver," Pike said. "Let's leave it as it is for now, Rose. My guess is they won't make a move until we're on the river. We won't have as many men then."

"Pike—"

"Let's talk about it later, Harley," Pike said. "Skins might have some ideas."

"All right."

"And let's keep this between us, for now," Pike added. "I don't want anyone going off half-cocked."

"All right," Rose said. "I'll see you later."

Pike left Rose's tent and headed for Sheila's. He wanted to make sure Donna had gotten settled in.

As Pike approached the tent Sheila came walking out. She stopped when she saw him and stood with her hands on her slim hips.

"Got a new one?"

"New what?" he asked.

"Woman."

"I don't have a woman, Sheila."

"I can understand that," she said, "the way you treat them."

"What are you—" Pike started, and then he realized that she was talking about Rita. "Look, Sheila—"

"You should take notice of the way your partner treats women, Pike," Sheila said, walking past him. "Your new one is inside."

"I don't *have* a new one," he said to her retreating back.

He shook his head and walked up to the tent.

"Donna?"

"Come on inside," she called.

He lifted the flap and entered. She turned to face him with her hands clasped behind her back. She was still bundled up against the cold, but her head was bare. Her hair looked clean, and he imagined he could smell it in the close confines of the tent.

"How are you doing?" he asked.

"Fine."

"Getting settled in?"

"Sure."

"What about Sheila . . ."

"She's great," Donna said. "I'll be comfortable here. It'll only be a couple of weeks."

"Right," Pike said, "a couple of weeks."

"Do you have the rest of your crews picked out yet?" she asked.

"No, not yet," Pike said. "Maybe you can help us out

with that. We've got a few men who have worked mackinaws before, but after that all we've got are volunteers. We're going to have to sort through them to find the ones who will work out, and then we've got a short time to teach them what they need to know."

"I'll help all I can," she said.

"How much do you know about mackinaws?"

She smiled and said, "Everything there is to know, Pike."

"Good," he said. "Right now, why don't we get you some coffee, and something to eat?"

"Sounds good to me."

CHAPTER ELEVEN

That night Pike, Skins, and Harley Rose ate with Sheila and Donna Lee in front of Rose's tent. Pike could see that Rose was impressed with Donna Lee. She talked about the mountains with assurance, impressing even McConnell, and Pike himself. Sheila stared at Donna while she spoke, but her face was flat and expressionless. She was allowing the girl to stay in her tent, but Sheila was, after all, Rita's friend, and thought that Donna was replacing Rita in Pike's affections.

Donna yawned over coffee and said, "Time to turn in." She looked at Sheila.

"You go ahead, Donna," Sheila said. "I'll clean up here."

"I'll help."

"Never mind," Sheila said, a little too sharply. "I'll take care of it."

Donna backed off and said, "All right."

"I'll walk you to your tent," Pike said, drawing a look from Sheila. He turned to Harley Rose and said,

"I'll be right back."

"Right."

As they walked Donna said, "Remember what I said to you earlier?"

"About what?"

"You asked me how Sheila was and I said she was fine?"

"Yeah?"

"I don't think she likes me."

"It's not your fault."

"Then whose is it?"

"Mine?"

"Oh?"

Pike told Donna about Rita and Donna listened, nodding her head.

"That explains it, I guess," Donna said. "Sheila thinks I'm replacing her friend."

"I guess so," Pike said. "I'm sorry about that."

"Don't be," Donna said. "It's been a while since I met an interesting man. I wouldn't mind replacing Rita for a while."

"What?" Pike said before he could stop himself.

"Was that too aggressive for you?" Donna asked. "To tell you the truth, I'd rather share your tent than Sheila's."

"Well," Pike said, rubbing his jaw, "that would suit Skins. He could move back in with Sheila."

"It seems I've put a few people out by coming here," Donna said.

"If you're serious about this," Pike said, "we can fix it."

She stopped and turned to face him, putting her hands on his chest.

"I'm serious."

"All right, then," he said. "Get your gear and move it to my tent. I'll take care of it."

"All right."

While Donna moved her stuff to Pike's tent Pike went back to Harley Rose's tent, pulled McConnell aside, and explained the situation to him.

"Suits me," McConnell said.

"I told her it would."

"I'll collect my gear in the morning," McConnell said. "I won't need it tonight."

"What about Sheila?"

"She won't mind."

"No, I mean . . ."

"Oh, you mean about Rita? Don't worry. I'll try and keep her occupied."

Pike smiled and said, "I'm sure you'll do more than try."

"Besides," McConnell said, "in another couple of weeks we'll be on our way."

"Right," Pike said. He'd been wondering about that. McConnell and Sheila had hit it off so well he wondered what his friend's plans would be once the skins were delivered downriver. This wasn't the time to ask him, though.

"I'll tell Sheila now."

"I'll put your gear aside. Tell Harley I'll be back. He wants to talk about this thing with LeConte."

"Yeah," McConnell said, "he mentioned Cal Devers. We should talk about it."

"I won't be long."

103

"I know you don't *intend* to be . . ." McConnell said with a smile.

Pike went to his tent and found Donna making herself at home. He collected McConnell's gear and set it aside in a corner of the tent.

"Well," she said, facing him, "this is going to be cozy."

"Yes."

"And warm," she said, "warmer than Sheila's tent."

Pike knew what she meant. Two bodies together created more heat than two bodies simply occupying the same tent.

"I think I'll turn in," she said, looking at him boldly.

"I, uh, have to go and talk to Harley and Skins for a while," Pike said, "but I'll be back soon."

She looked disappointed, but said that she would wait.

"I might fall asleep."

"I don't blame you—"

"Wake me up when you get back," she said, "will you?"

"Oh," he said, "sure."

Rita watched as Pike left his tent, leaving the woman inside. She knew that Pike had brought Donna here to replace her. Tears stung her eyes because she couldn't understand why. What had she done to deserve this? Why were men always leaving her?

*****

104

When Pike returned to Harley Rose's tent, Sheila was gone. Rose and McConnell were having coffee, and as Pike approached, McConnell poured him one and handed it to him.

"Where's Sheila?" Pike asked.

"She went back to the tent to, uh, warm up the blankets."

"Don't you fellas find women a distraction?" Rose asked.

Pike and McConnell exchanged a glance, and then they both said, "Yes."

Rose shook his head.

"I'm glad I'm not a ladies' man. My life is much simpler."

McConnell raised his cup and said, "To the simple life."

"Life would be even simpler if we didn't have to worry about Cal Devers."

"I know Devers," McConnell said.

"Yeah," Pike said, "we both know Devers."

"What have you got against Devers?" Rose asked. "I mean, besides the fact that he's a thief and a liar."

"I know him," McConnell said, "but he's never done me any harm."

Rose looked at Pike and knew instinctively that the big man couldn't say the same thing.

"So what's your story?" Rose asked.

"It's not a long one," Pike said. "A few years back I was hunting with a man named Tom Seidman."

"I knew Seidman."

"Knew," Pike said, "right. I went out one day to check traps and when I came back Seidman was dead and our skins were gone."

"Devers?"

"That's right."

"Could you prove it?"

"No," Pike said, "but Devers sold a big cache of beaver at rendezvous that year."

"Maybe he caught them himself?"

Pike looked at Rose and said, "Cal Devers never worked that hard in his life."

Rose looked at McConnell, who just shrugged his shoulders.

"He's stolen from others," Pike said.

"That doesn't prove he did it to you, or that he killed Seidman."

"He did it," Pike said.

"Did you approach him?"

Pike didn't answer.

"Pike gave Devers a pretty bad beating at rendezvous that year."

"I haven't seen him since," Pike said. "If I do, I'll kill him."

McConnell had dealt with Pike's brand of vengeance before, and he knew that Pike meant what he said. His thirst for revenge where Devers was concerned was not such that Pike was actively hunting the man, but McConnell knew that Pike meant what he said. If Cal Devers ever crossed his path again, the man would not survive it.

Cal Devers rubbed his left side as he looked down at the camp below him. He could still remember the pain Pike's fists had caused him a few years ago.

He heard a sound behind him and turned to watch as

Sandy Dunlap approached.

"It's about time," Devers said.

Dunlap was one of the men Henri LeConte had hired. He was a big man, not tall but thick, heavy without being fat. He was in his thirties, and Devers had used him before a couple of times.

"Keep a sharp eye out, Dunlap."

"What am I supposed to be looking for?" Dunlap asked as he relieved Devers.

"Just keep watchin'," Devers said. "I'll be back after I get somethin' to eat."

Dunlap shrugged and looked down at the camp. It looked like any other camp he had seen before, except larger. He didn't know what was going on, all he knew was that he and the others would be making some good money from this job, maybe even a hundred dollars apiece.

Sandy Dunlap could do a lot with a hundred dollars.

Devers mounted his horse and took one last look at Dunlap. The man typified the kind of help he had told LeConte to go out and get. Men not too bright. Smart enough to follow orders, dumb enough to do it cheap.

There was no need to spread *too* much of the wealth out.

Pike walked slowly to his tent. He hadn't thought about Cal Devers in a while, and now that he was he was getting all steamed up again about the man. He knew he should have hunted him down years ago and killed him. Everyone kept telling him—like Harley Rose did—that he couldn't prove that Devers slit Tom Seidman's throat while Seidman was asleep. Damn

Seidman anyway for taking up drinking at such a late age. He'd waited until he was fifty to make a habit of it, and that night he'd been so drunk he hadn't heard Devers sneak into camp. In fact, maybe he never knew what had happened to him, but Pike knew, and Pike knew who did it, proof or no proof.

When he reached his tent he stopped before flipping the flap aside. Donna Lee was waiting for him inside, and he wanted to leave the memory of what Cal Devers had done out here so that it wouldn't come between them.

When he stepped inside, Donna sat up from the floor, where she had made a bed from blankets. She looked very pretty sitting there with her short hair slightly mussed and an almost embarrassed look on her face.

"I waited up," she said, sleepily. From the looks of her eyes, she couldn't have waited much longer.

He smiled at her and said, "I'm glad you did."

CHAPTER TWELVE

Pike undressed while Donna watched, and then she tossed aside the blanket she was hiding behind to show him her body. It was a fine body, not as full as Rita's, but her breasts were round and firm, and her pink nipples were already hardening.

He slid into her arms and she pressed her hot body up against him.

"You're cold," she said. She reached for the blanket and pulled it over them. "I'll warm you up."

"I'm warm already."

"I'll warm you more," she said, pressing her hot mouth against his neck. He felt a tongue like velvet slide over his skin, down his throat to his chest, where it circled his nipples.

One of her hands slid down between them and took hold of him, and she moaned appreciatively.

"I see you're a big man in more ways than one," she murmured.

Her tongue traced a wet trail over his belly until her head was down between his legs. They weren't under the blanket anymore as her mouth came down around him, engulfing him in its heat, and this time he moaned and reached down to cup her head.

She sucked him noisily, obviously enjoying it, and when he was swollen to bursting she stopped and straddled him, taking him inside of her.

He played with her breasts while she rode him, squeezing them, popping the nipples between his fingers. She braced her hands on his chest while she increased her speed, her head thrown back and little moans escaping from her once in a while.

He slid his hands down her back to cup her buttocks and she laid the length of herself down on him so he could run his hands over her smooth ass.

She kissed him then, her tongue blooming in his mouth like a sweet flower. She liked slow, long, wet kissing, which suited him just fine, because her mouth was full and she tasted like sugar to him.

He cupped her face in his hands, driving his tongue deep into her mouth. He could feel her hard nipples scraping his chest, and then suddenly he erupted inside of her and she pressed her mouth more tightly against his, as if trying to suffocate him. Her moans and cries were muffled in his mouth and he reached for her ass again and squeezed it hard as he shot the last of his seed into her.

Most women he'd known usually quit after that, but she kept after him, using her mouth on him until he was swollen full again, and then he was on top of her, bulling his way into her. She wrapped her legs around his waist and reached for his buttocks. It took longer the second time, which neither of them seemed to mind. The tent filled with the smell of their sweat and sex, and

110

their mingled moans and cries which soon became grunts and groans as they strained harder and harder against each other. When he exploded into her this time he roared like a wounded animal. Her insides seemed to suck his ejaculation from him this time, and it was painful and wonderful at the same time.

After that she let him sleep, but not for long. . . .

"Jesus," he said after their third coupling, "how long has it been for you, or are you always like that?"

"Like what?"

He turned his head to look at her. She was lying on her back next to him, glistening with sweat, running the fingers of her right hand back and forth over her breasts absently.

"Hungry."

She smiled, and then laughed and looked at him.

"You struck me as pretty hungry, yourself, and I'll bet it ain't been that long for you."

Not that long at all, he thought, remembering the last time he and Rita had been in here together.

"You're not tired, are you?" she asked.

"Dead tired," he said.

She put her hand on his belly, and then slid it lower until she had him in her hand. His penis was only semi-erect, and he thought it would take some attention from her mouth to get him ready again. She seemed content, however, just to lie there with him in her hand, and before long she fell asleep like that.

And so did he.

*****

When they woke in the morning they made love again, and then he was ready for a cup of coffee.

"Get me one, too, will you, Pike?" she said, stretching sleepily. "If I fall asleep again, wake me when you get back with it?"

Well, if he thought she was going to wait on him the way Rita did, it appeared he was in for a surprise.

He got up, got dressed, and went out to get the coffee.

John Blackburn hated Pike more this morning then he ever had.

The night before, knowing that Pike had kicked Rita out, he had gone to Rita's tent and told her how he felt about her. He had felt it was time.

She turned him away, vehemently.

"You men are all alike," she said, "and I'll have nothing to do with any of you, ever again."

That was Pike's fault. If he had left her alone, and let her get over the hurt her husband had caused her, Blackburn might have been able to win her over.

He watched as Pike came out of his tent and walked over to one of the fires where coffee was on.

Blackburn was still burning also about McConnell finding out how he felt about the water. He knew that he was going to have to get over that fear if he was going to go down the Missouri in a mackinaw, and he was determined to do it. Damned if he'd show Pike he was afraid.

Damn Pike to hell, he'd show him he wasn't afraid of water, of him, or of nothing!

*****

Rita watched as Pike exited his tent, and smirked. It looked like his new woman wasn't willing to get him coffee. He was probably already sorry he had taken up with her, but Rita wouldn't take him back.

Not ever.

Sandy Dunlap rubbed his eyes and stared down at the camp, which was starting to show signs of life. Damn Devers, anyway. The man said he'd be right back after he had some dinner, and Dunlap had ended up spending the night out here in the cold.

Only the thought of a hundred dollars kept Dunlap from just walking off.

"Dunlap is going to be angry, *mon ami,*" LeConte said, staring at Devers over a cup of coffee.

"He's gettin' paid more than he ever has for a job," Devers said. "That'll keep him from gettin' too damned angry."

"Still," LeConte said, "you will have to explain—"

"No," Devers said, "I won't have to explain, Henri, you will."

"I?"

"You're gonna relieve him," Devers said.

"Why me?"

"Because I'm gonna scout the river edge for a likely place for us to make our move—unless you want to do it?" Devers asked.

LeConte shook his head. He freely admitted that Devers was the planner of the two.

"I will relieve Dunlap," LeConte said, standing up,

113

"just make sure someone relieves me before too long."

"I'll send one of these other idiots to relieve you soon," Devers promised.

The other "idiots" were still asleep in their blankets. The Indians, however, were awake. They were Snake Indians, half a dozen of them, and they had been promised all sorts of trinkets for their help—and whiskey. With them and the other men LeConte had hired, they were a dozen strong, more than enough to take care of two mackinaws full of men stuck out in the middle of a river.

Devers figured they would either force the mackinaws to shore, or kill the men while the boats were still on the river, and then retrieve the drifting boats themselves.

The key, of course, was that no one in the camp was aware that they were being watched.

As Pike headed back to the tent with two cups of coffee he risked a look around, using just his eyes and not raising his head at all. If he wanted to keep an eye on this camp, where would he set up? He came up with two possibilities, and wondered if he and McConnell shouldn't check it out later on.

Right now, though, he had something more pressing to take care of.

McConnell reached up and rubbed his hands over Sheila's small breasts. She moaned as his palms pressed against her nipples while she rode him, and then her breath caught as she experienced her first climax of the morning. Moments later, McConnell groaned as he exploded into her, and then she collapsed on him.

"Why is your friend such a shit?"

"Which friend is that?"

She pinched him and said, "You know who. Pike."

"Who says he's a shit?"

"I do."

"Why?"

"Look how he's treated Rita."

"He sure hasn't treated her as bad as her husband did," McConnell pointed out. "Her husband left her. Pike's still here."

"Flaunting another woman under her nose."

"Pike didn't bring Donna Lee back here to flaunt her at anyone."

"Did you agree to bring her back?"

"Sure I did," McConnell said.

"Why?"

"We need experienced hands on the mackinaws, and she has the experience."

She lifted her head and looked at him.

"Is that the only reason?"

He made circles on her butt with his palms and said, "That's the only reason."

She crawled up further on him so she could kiss him, her tongue fluttering teasingly on his lips without entering his mouth.

"But Pike is still a shit."

McConnell decided not to argue. When a woman is mad at a man for the ways he's treated another woman, an argument was useless.

Women were like that.

*****

"Come back in here," Donna said from inside the blankets. She was sitting up with a cup of coffee in her hand. This morning her short hair was more than just a little tousled. Pike thought she looked very fetching, and it wasn't easy to refuse her.

"I've got work to do," Pike said. "We were supposed to start picking our men last night, and I ended up doing something else."

"Oh?" she said. "With who?"

He ignored her.

"I've got to find Rose and apologize, so we can get started talking to the men today. I want to come out of today with two mackinaw crews, and start working with them tomorrow."

"All right," she said, running one hand through her hair. "I'll get dressed and help."

"Actually," he said, standing up, "we won't need your help until after we pick out the men, so if you want you can stay inside for a while longer. Once you leave those warm blankets, you aren't going to find another warm spot."

"Hmm," she said, "you have a point. I think I'll take your advice."

She held the empty cup out to him and he took it, leaning over to kiss her before straightening. Her mouth was warm and she smelled of coffee now.

She lay back down, burrowing deep into the blankets, and said, "See you for lunch, Pike."

Pike looked down at her for a moment, then shook his head and forced himself to leave.

It wasn't one of the easiest things he had ever done in his life.

CHAPTER THIRTEEN

It took the better part of the day to interview all of the men in camp to see if they had any experience on a mackinaw. They only found four men who said that they had *been* in a mackinaw, one of them only once, "And I got sick," he had admitted.

Pike, McConnell, and Rose discussed the situation while they waited for dinner to be ready.

"With Skins, Donna, and myself, we've got seven people who have been on a mackinaw," Pike said. "Of the seven, I think there may be four of us who actually know what we're doing."

"If Donna is telling the truth," McConnell said.

"What?" Pike said.

"Well . . . we don't know that she's ever *really* been on a mackinaw," McConnell said. "We only have her word for it."

Pike stared at McConnell, wondering how much of what he had just said came from Sheila. He had never seen a woman have as much of an effect on his friend.

"I guess we'll find out for sure when we pick up the

mackinaws," Pike said. He looked at Rose. "We're going to need four oarsmen and a steersman for each boat, and I think we should have one more man as a lookout. Skins can act as steersman on one boat, and I will do the same on the other. The other five that we have will act as oarsmen. That means we need five more people—three oarsmen and two lookouts—preferably two men who can shoot."

"Still expecting trouble, eh?" Rose asked.

"I think we should plan on it," Pike said, and McConnell nodded.

"Well," Rose said, "we've got eight men who said they're willing to try their hand on the boat."

"Well, the lookout job is easy enough," McConnell said. "All we have to do is come up with three oarsmen."

"Blackie could be one of the lookouts," Rose said. Pike thought Rose's tone was a little hopeful. "He can shoot well enough."

"What about the water?" McConnell asked.

Rose said, "He really wants to go."

"He can come with us to pick up the mackinaws," Pike said. "We should be able to tell something just on the trip from the boatyard to here."

"I'll tell him," Rose said.

"All right," Pike said.

They heard the sound of Sheila banging a wooden spoon against the bottom of a pot, signaling that dinner was ready.

"After dinner," Pike said, "we'll pick out our other lookout, and our three oarsmen."

"Suits me," Rose said, standing up. "Let's eat."

Rose rushed ahead of them while Pike put his hand

118

on McConnell's arm to slow him down.

"What's going on?" he asked.

"Whataya mean?"

"Why are you running Donna down?"

"I'm not running her down," McConnell said. "I was just stating a fact. We only have her word—"

"We only have the word of the other men who claim to be experienced, also," Pike said. "Why didn't you challenge them?"

McConnell opened his mouth, then closed it, then said, "Uh, she's new to the camp, Pike. These other fellas have been here all along."

Pike frowned. He wanted to ask McConnell who was talking, him or Sheila, but he didn't want to put his friend in that position, so he decided to hold his tongue.

"I guess time will have to tell with all of them," Pike said.

"I guess so."

McConnell moved ahead of Pike, to where Sheila was holding a full plate out to him. Sheila cooked, but did not serve, as everyone simply grabbed a plate and took their own food—except for McConnell. Sheila always served him his plate, and then took one of her own. They then walked off and ate together.

Pike collected his plate and saw Donna walking over from the tent. He hadn't seen her all day, until now.

She got herself a plate of stew and went over to sit with him.

"How did it go?"

"Fairly well," he said. "We've got three experienced oarsmen, and another man who's done it once. We need three more."

"Well, good," Donna said. She ate her stew while looking all around her. "I'm afraid this is my first good look at the camp. I sort of stayed inside all day." She looked over at him and added, "For some reason I felt pretty wore out."

"I can't imagine why."

"There are really a lot of people here," she said, looking around at the women and children as well as the hunters. Three small children went running by, laughing, chasing one another, while their mothers shouted for them to come and eat. Donna laughed, then saw someone staring at them from across the way.

"Who is that woman?"

Pike looked where she was indicating and saw Rita sitting alone, staring across at them. He couldn't really tell which of them she was staring at, but the effect was the same.

"Her name is Rita."

Donna looked at Pike and said, "Friend of yours? Oh, wait, that's Sheila's friend, isn't it? The one you, uh . . ."

"Yeah," Pike said, "she's the one."

Donna looked at Rita again.

"Ooh," she said, shivering, "I know it's cold out here, but her stare is even colder."

"Don't worry about it," Pike said. "I'm sorry you have to—"

"Hey, don't apologize," she said, cutting him off. "I sort of bulled my way in here, remember . . . and in more ways than one, too."

He grinned and said, "I remember."

"This stew is good," she said. "Who cooks here?"

"A few of the women cook," Pike said. "Sheila made this stew."

Donna stopped chewing for a moment and said, "You don't think she'd poison me, do you?"

"I don't think so," he said, as she started to chew again. "She'd have to poison everyone to get to you, and I don't think she's prepared to do that."

"Good," Donna said, "then I can go and get myself another plate. Excuse me."

Pike watched as she walked over to the fire and scooped herself out another helping. He expected her to turn around and walk back toward him, but she surprised him. She kept right on walking and didn't stop until she was standing in front of Rita.

Pike held his breath while Donna and Rita carried on a conversation that only lasted about a minute, and then Donna turned and walked back to Pike. She sat down next to him and proceeded to eat as if nothing had happened. Pike looked at Rita and saw that she was glancing around, looking over at them now only occasionally, instead of glaring as she had been.

"What was that all about?" he asked Donna.

"I just told her that I didn't like to be stared at," Donna said.

Pike marveled at Donna's aggressiveness. She had demonstrated it to him in many ways. First, asking to go along on the mackinaw, and then crawling into his blankets with him—and now, confronting Rita, a much larger woman, the way she had, and apparently getting the better of the exchange.

Donna saw him staring at her and asked, "What's the matter?"

121

"Nothing," he said, "I just find you a little bit amazing."

She smiled broadly and said, "That's it? Just a little bit? Give me time."

"We've got some of that," he said, "but not much."

"Well," she said, "we'll just have to make do with what we have."

After dinner Donna said she wanted to take a walk around the camp, maybe meet some of the people.

"Don't get into trouble," he said.

She frowned at him mightily and said, "Trouble is my middle name."

He watched her walk away, then looked around for McConnell and Rose. Once or twice during dinner he had sneaked a glance at the high ground at the two places he would have picked as vantage points. He never did spot anyone, but they had to be up there.

McConnell and Sheila seemed to have gotten lost. Apparently when a woman cooked, some of the others cleaned. He hadn't noticed that before. The women in camp seemed to have the chores divvied up pretty efficiently.

He saw Rose talking to a couple of the men who had volunteered as apprentice oarsmen, and he walked over to join them.

"Pike," Rose said, "this here is Buck Styles and Pat Lobro."

Styles was a big man in his forties with bulging biceps and a hard paunch. Lobro, much smaller, in his thirties, still appeared to be in excellent physical shape.

"I was thinking that your oarsmen should probably be in the best possible shape," Rose said.

"That's a fact," Pike said.

"Styles and Lobro fit that bill, and they're willing to learn."

"I always wanted to work a mackinaw," Lobro said, "I just never had the chance."

"Well, you've got it now," Pike said. He looked at Rose and said, "Why don't I just leave the choice of the third man up to you, as well? And Blackburn will be one of the lookouts. We need another."

"I'll take care of that, too, if it's okay with you," Rose said. "I've got someone in mind."

"A good shot?"

"The best in camp."

"All right, then," Pike said, "we're all set." He looked at the other two men and said, "Oarsman lessons start in the morning."

Both men nodded and walked off, talking to each other animatedly. They both seemed anxious to get started.

"Harley, we've got to pick out a spot along the river here for us to bring the boats into shore and load the skins," Pike said. "You want to ride out with me and have a look?"

"Now?"

"We've still got about an hour of daylight," Pike said. "Why not put it to good use."

"I'll get my horse," Rose said. "I'll meet you back here."

"Saddle mine, too, will you?" Pike asked. "And meet me here in ten minutes? I want to find Skins."

"I saw him and Sheila head back to her tent."

"That's what I thought," Pike said. "I'll have to interrupt them."

"Like I told you boys before," Rose said, "women can be a distraction. I've also seen friends fall out over them more times than I care to count."

"I understand what you're saying, Harley," Pike said. "I think Skins and I have known each other too long for that to be a problem."

Rose shook his head, said, "Women," and went to get his horse.

"Skins?" Pike called outside of Sheila's tent.

"Yeah?" his friend called from inside.

"Can I see you a minute?"

"Sure."

He heard some rustling from inside, and some urgent whispering—most of which seemed to be being done by Sheila. She sounded as if she was complaining. Finally, Skins stuck his head out of the tent.

"Whatsamatter?" he asked.

"Harley and I are going to ride down by the river," Pike said. "I want to see if we can find a spot to load the boats."

"Good idea," McConnell said. "Do you want me to come along?"

"No," Pike said, "I want you to follow us, and see what you can see."

"I get it," McConnell said. "Somebody watchin' you might get careless and let *me* see *them.*"

"Right," Pike said. "I've been looking at the high

ground around here, and there's a couple of spots I'd pick out if I wanted to keep an eye on this camp."

"Yeah," McConnell said, "I've done the same. We probably picked the same two spots."

"Give us five minutes, and then follow," Pike said, then added, "that is, if it isn't a problem?"

McConnell frowned and said, "Why would it be a problem?"

"It's not," Pike said, shrugging, "if you say it's not."

"I'll do my part, Pike," McConnell said. "I always do, don't I?"

"Yep," Pike said, "you do. See you later, when we get back."

"Right."

"Oh," Pike said, "if you do see anyone, don't do anything, all right?"

"I'll just spot 'em," McConnell said. "If we know where they are, and they don't *know* that we know, we'll have the upper hand."

"Right."

"Anything else you want to talk about?" McConnell asked.

Pike hesitated, then said, "Yeah, there is, but it will wait until later."

"Okay," McConnell said. "Be careful out there."

"You, too."

McConnell withdrew and Pike walked away, shaking his head. The whole conversation had seemed strained, and he didn't like it. Although he and McConnell had ridden together a lot, they had also ridden alone.

Maybe it was time to split up again, for a while.

*****

Inside the tent, while McConnell dressed, Sheila tried to talk him out of going.

"Why do you always let him tell you what to do?" she demanded.

"I don't."

"Yes, you do."

"Then if I do," he said, looking at her, "it's because he's right."

"Someone else could do it."

He stared at her and said, "Not as well as I can." He'd had plenty of practice watching Pike's back, and Pike had returned the favor many times over.

"There's somethin' you don't understand, Sheila," McConnell said. "Pike is my friend."

"And what am I?"

"You're someone I met months ago," he said. "Pike is someone I know for years."

"And your friend is more important than I am?" she asked. As if to make his reply even more difficult she got to her knees, so that the blankets fell away from her nakedness. Her slender body was taut and unblemished, possibly the loveliest thing he'd ever seen. Her breasts were small and hard, her nipples pink. Her belly was flat, and the cleft of her navel was dark. Below it was a little trail of fine, golden, downy hairs that led to a heavy bush between her legs.

"You're choosin' to put it that way," McConnell said, fully dressed now, "not me. My relationship with Pike is one thing, and the way I feel about you is another." He picked up his rifle and walked to the tent flap.

"Well," she said, "you just might have to choose."

He stopped short of leaving and looked at her.

"Sheila, Rita's problem with Pike—and with *men*—is hers, not yours."

"Rita's my friend!" Sheila said.

He smiled at her and said, "See? Think about what you just said while I'm away."

She opened her mouth to reply, then stopped herself short as he left.

She hated to admit it, but he had a point.

CHAPTER FOURTEEN

Pike and Harley Rose rode down to the river's edge and discovered that finding a spot to load was not difficult at all—not at this point in the river.

"It's pretty shallow here," Rose said, pointing. "We won't be able to bring the boats too far into shore, but we'll be able to wade out to them."

Pike nodded his agreement. He was paying attention to what Rose was saying, but he was also trying to pay attention to his instincts.

At that moment, his instincts were telling him that they were being watched.

When Henri LeConte saw Pike and the other man leaving the camp, he wondered where they could be going. Since they didn't have any supplies with them, it couldn't have been very far. He decided to abandon the camp and keep an eye on them.

He mounted his horse and followed behind them, trying to keep them in sight without letting them see him. LeConte was an excellent tracker, the best he knew of, and he had great faith in his ability to do just that.

McConnell followed the sign left by Pike and Harley Rose. His mind kept wandering to his tiff with Sheila, and he had to shake himself several times to pay attention to what he was doing. He had never let a woman interfere with him in this way before. He certainly had never let a woman affect his friendship with Pike before, and he didn't like that he was doing it now. He and Pike had been friends for a lot of years, and more than that. When you've saved someone's life as many times as he and Pike had done for each other, it made for something deeper than friendship. McConnell didn't think that a word had been invented yet to describe his relationship with Pike.

He liked Sheila, maybe more than any other woman he had ever known. Most of the time she was sweet and considerate, and they usually agreed on everything—and they were especially compatible when it came to sex. Her friendship with Rita, however, had affected the way she felt about Pike, and she was trying to drive a wedge between Pike and McConnell.

McConnell certainly wouldn't have tried to do that with her and Rita.

He shook his head again and looked around him. When he looked at the ground he noticed something and drew his horse in.

He had been following sign left by two men, but he was now looking at sign left by three, one riding behind the other two.

Pike was right again.

*****

"Let's go back to camp a different way," Pike said to Rose.

"Why?"

"I've got McConnell riding drag on us."

"Why?" Rose asked, again. "Oh, you mean to check and see if we're followed?"

"Right."

"And if we are?"

"He's just going to watch," Pike said. "Come on, it'll be dark soon. I think it's a pretty safe bet that we can load the boats here."

Rose nodded, and they started back to camp by a different route.

LeConte frowned.

He had been prepared to take cover when Pike and Rose retraced their steps to camp, but they seemed to be returning by a different route. Why would they do that—unless they knew someone was behind them?

Suddenly, LeConte felt exposed, naked. He turned in his saddle and looked behind. He didn't see anyone, but that didn't mean that no one was there.

He had a choice to make now. Follow Pike back to camp, or return to his vantage point on his own. He felt sure that what Pike and the other man had been doing was checking the river for a location where they could load their boats. That done, and darkness falling, they'd be heading back to camp for sure. No point in following them. What was left for him to do, then, was return to his high ground, finding out along the way if

131

he had been followed.

He didn't think anyone could follow him without his knowing it, but he wasn't going to take any chances. He turned his horse and retraced his steps.

As McConnell had expected, Pike and Rose were taking a different route back to camp.

McConnell had found himself some high ground from where he could not only see them, but the man who was following them, as well. He could have been wrong, but he didn't think he was. The man following them looked like the Frenchman he had seen at Fort Pierre.

The Frenchman turned his horse now and was retracing his steps rather than continuing to follow Pike. As he rode, he seemed to be watching the ground.

Somehow, the Frenchman had figured out what was happening, that while he was following Pike and Rose, *he* was being followed. He was checking for the sign left by McConnell.

McConnell knew that if the man was good enough there was no way he *wouldn't* be able to see his sign. There was nothing he could do about that. What he had to do now was follow the man and find out *where* he was watching the camp from.

One thing was almost certain. The man now knew that they knew about him.

Whatever advantage they might have had before, when that was not the case, was gone.

*****

Pike saw McConnell riding into camp after dark and walked out to meet him.

"Are you all right?"

"Fine," McConnell said. He dismounted and handed his horse over to someone. "I'll unsaddle him myself in a minute," he told the man, who nodded.

"Did you see him?" Pike asked.

"Looked like the same man from Fort Pierre," McConnell said, "but he knows we know about him."

"How?"

McConnell explained his theory to Pike.

"That's my fault," Pike said, frowning. "We should have taken the same route back."

"Can't do anything about that now."

"Well," Pike said, "now they know that we know they're watching us."

"You think that will change their plans at all?" McConnell asked.

"I doubt it," Pike said. "They've got too much invested in us—and if we *are* dealing with Devers, he's not going to give up."

"I guess not," McConnell said. "I have to take care of my horse."

"Skins," Pike said, "can we talk later?"

"Sure," McConnell said, "but I think I know what you want to talk about."

"I'll buy you a cup of coffee after you've cared for your horse."

McConnell smiled and said, "Deal."

LeConte was finally relieved just after dark, and

rode back to camp, angry.

"I was supposed to be relieved earlier," he told Devers.

"Never mind that," Devers said. "Tell me what went on today."

LeConte frowned. He wondered if Devers was just trying to show everyone who was in charge. He didn't need to do that. Everyone knew that he was the planner, but that didn't mean that he had to treat LeConte the way he treated the others. After all, they were supposed to be partners.

He told Devers what had happened, and explained what he thought.

"I agree," Devers said, "they know they're being watched."

"So what do we do now?"

"Nothing," Devers said, "nothing different, that is. We'll go according to plan."

"What plan?"

Devers grinned and said, "The one I came up with today. Come on, I'll explain it to you. . . ."

CHAPTER FIFTEEN

For the third time Pike was preparing to ride from camp to Fort Pierre. This time he was taking both mackinaw crews with him.

It was decided that Pike would run one crew, consisting of Donna, Lobro, Styles, Matt Christopher—the good shot Rose had mentioned—and a man named Joe Rand. Christopher would be the lookout, while the others worked the oars. Pike would be the steersman.

On the other mackinaw, steersman McConnell would have oarsmen Paul Exman, Wally Dennis, Tom Gary, and Mike Collins. The lookout would be Blackburn.

The morning they were to leave, Pike and Donna woke very early. They had not made love that night, but had slept in each other's arms. Now, when they woke, they dressed quickly and went outside. They had hot cups of coffee warming their hands and bellies when McConnell came from his tent. By ones and twos the other men joined them, Blackburn and Harley Rose being last. Blackburn did not look happy, and

Pike suspected that Rose had been telling the man something he didn't want to hear very much.

When everyone had some hot coffee in them three men went to get everyone's horses, and then pack the mules.

"You figure we'll be followed," McConnell said.

"I don't think so," Pike said. "Not this time. They pretty much know where we're going, and they've got no reason to hit us now. No, unless we run into some Indians, I think this trip to Fort Pierre will be pretty uneventful."

The men with the horses arrived. They were also leading three pack mules that had been loaded with skins for the roofs of the mackinaws. Pike and the two crews would remain in Fort Pierre for two nights, and pick up the boats in the morning or early afternoon of the third day. That would give the boatyard plenty of time to finish the mackinaws.

"Are we all ready?" Pike called out, and everyone answered affirmatively.

"Good luck," Rose said, reaching up to shake Pike's hand. "We'll be watching the river for you."

"I don't figure we'll be more than three days, four at the most."

"We'll be ready."

"And be on your guard," Pike warned.

"Don't worry," Rose said, "we will."

Pike waved, and then led the group out of camp single file. The next to last man—Joe Rand—led the mules, and Matt Christopher brought up the rear.

"I told you they'd leave today," Devers said to

LeConte. He had seen them stacking the skins they'd need for the mackinaws the day before, and that had led him to believe that this was the day they would head for Fort Pierre to pick up the boats.

"Are we going to follow them?" LeConte asked.

"No," Devers said, "we know where they're headed. We'll just wait here for them to come back on the river. Three days, four at the most. Then we let them load and get under way."

"And spring our trap, eh?"

"And spring our trap," Devers said, "when the time is right."

Pike wondered if his brain was going weak on him. It only took a few hours for him to realize that it was going to take two full days to get to Fort Pierre. The fact that there were twelve of them riding, and that they had three heavily laden mules with them, slowed them down considerably. He should have realized that before they started out.

"It'll be five days before we get back," Pike said to McConnell.

"Don't worry about it," McConnell said. "One more day won't make a difference. Harley will probably figure it out for himself."

"I'm just annoyed that I didn't realize it myself," Pike said.

"Nobody's perfect, Pike."

"Especially me."

Pike had made a lot of mistakes over the past few months. Maybe the biggest was not riding out of Harley Rose's camp the same hour they had ridden in.

Since then he'd made mistakes with John Blackburn, Rita, he'd even made some with Skins. He'd probably made enemies out of Blackburn and Rita, which was stupid, because he had all the enemies he needed in his life.

Now he'd made a mistake in figuring their time to and from Fort Pierre.

He decided that he'd better get his head on straight in a hurry—especially with someone stalking them, intending to try to steal their skins.

The next mistake he made might be fatal.

They rode into Fort Pierre two days later. Pike didn't even bother stopping in the settlement. He led them right through it to the boatyard, where they unloaded the skins under the watchful eye of Jamie Pebbles.

"Did we bring enough?" McConnell asked.

"Plenty," Pebbles said. "Today bein' Monday, your mackinaws will be ready by Wednesday mornin'."

"We'll be here to pick them up," Pike promised.

"And pay the rest of the money?"

"And pay the rest of the money," Pike said. The two men shook hands and Pebbles turned and went into the yard.

Now that the skins were unloaded the other men had gone to find someplace to camp for two nights, and then they'd probably end up at Hillerman's trading post, looking for something to eat and drink—which didn't sound like a bad idea.

Pike looked around and saw that Donna Lee had not

waited for him. He didn't mind that. She was a damned sight less possessive than Rita had been, and he needed that in a woman just about now.

"Where to?" McConnell asked.

"A beer," Pike said, "and then we can figure out how we're going to pass today and tomorrow, until it's time to pick up the boats."

"We *could* play poker," McConnell said.

"That's right." Pike was an excellent poker player. "We *could* do that."

They started walking back to the settlement, leading their horses.

"What I mean is," McConnell went on, "you could play poker while I watch."

"All we have to do is find some men who want to play," Pike said.

"Hey," McConnell said, "we brought ten men with us—I mean, nine men and one woman. Some of them are bound to want to play."

"I doubt that any of them have money to play poker with."

"They don't need money."

"Oh?" Pike said. "And what will they play with? Buffalo chips?"

"The same thing you have to play with," McConnell said, a crafty look on his face.

"I've seen that look before," Pike said. "What are you up to?"

"Nothin'," McConnell said innocently. "All I'm sayin' is we've got a lot of skins to take downriver, and we all have our shares comin'."

"Are you saying I should put my shares up against

theirs and play them for them?"

"Our shares," McConnell said. "We're partners, remember?"

"We're all supposed to be partners in this."

"But we've all got our own shares comin' to us," McConnell said.

"And how do you intend to get them to agree to play for theirs?"

McConnell grinned and said, "Just leave that to me."

CHAPTER SIXTEEN

They all went to Hillerman's for lunch, a drink, or both, and Jim Hillerman was grateful for the business. So grateful, in fact, that he told Pike and McConnell that their food and drink was on him.

"Thanks, Jim," Pike said, raising his beer mug to the man.

"Least I can do, you bringin' me all this business, lately."

"Tell me something, Jim."

"What?"

"You ever see that Frenchman around here after we left last time?"

Hillerman shook his head. If it was possible, his hair seemed to have gotten shorter and the lower portion of his face wider and longer. "Never did see him again," he said. "Did you?"

"No," Pike said, "no, we never did."

"Maybe he was just passin' through, like he said," Hillerman said.

"Maybe," Pike said. "Thanks, Jim."

"What'd you ask him that for?" McConnell asked as Hillerman walked away to deal with a customer.

"Just confirming that he was here because of us," Pike said.

"Well, that seems to clinch it."

"Yeah."

McConnell looked behind them, where the other men and Donna Lee had taken tables and were eating and drinking. Donna seemed to be fitting in with them very nicely.

"Don't you think it's time we told them that somebody might be waitin' for us downriver?" McConnell asked.

Pike glanced over his shoulder, then looked back at McConnell.

"I'll tell them," he said, "just before we shove off."

"Pike?"

"Hmm?"

"When's the last time you were on a mackinaw?"

Pike looked at his friend.

"Same as you," he said. "Back in '34, when we went downriver with Jim Bridger."

"Not since then, huh?"

"Don't worry, Skins," Pike said. "It ain't something you forget."

"I hope not."

Pike was not as dubious as his friend about stepping foot in a mackinaw again. While they were working with the men, teaching them how to be oarsmen, Pike had found the memory of being on a mackinaw coming back to him. It was so entirely different from traveling by horseback that he found himself looking forward to it again.

"Where are you going?" he asked as McConnell turned away from the counter.

"I'm gonna join the fun," he said, "and try to set up that poker game for tonight."

Pike turned and leaned his elbows on the counter, watching his friend wade into the fray. In a corner, sitting by himself, was John Blackburn. He was nursing a mug of beer, taking turns staring into it, and then sipping at it without interest.

Pike still wasn't happy about Blackburn being along, even if he was on McConnell's boat. He didn't trust Blackburn to do what had to be done when the chips were down—namely, what he was told.

Pike decided to go out for a walk, maybe even down by the boatyard. It'd be interesting to watch them work on the mackinaws for a while.

Jamie Pebbles had no objection to Pike watching as he and his men worked on the mackinaws. The boats appeared to be finished except for the roofing, which was what the skins were for. He watched as they wet the skins and then affixed them to the roof of one of the mackinaws. Pike would have thought they'd let them dry first, but one of the men explained that it was better to let the skins dry and harden right on the boat.

He watched while they worked on one, and when it was obvious that they wouldn't get to the other one until the next day he decided to leave. It was almost dark by the time he got back to the settlement.

He went to Hillerman's and found only McConnell and three or four men still there. He didn't see Donna, and wondered where she had gone off to.

143

Hillerman was standing behind the counter, and Pike walked over and asked for a beer.

"I'll pay for this one."

"No argument from me," Hillerman said.

When Pike had his beer Hillerman leaned his elbows on the countertop and spoke.

"Skins seems to have worked up a poker game for you," he said.

"It's something to pass the time."

"That fella with the black beard seems to think it's more'n that."

Pike looked over where McConnell was sitting and didn't see who Hellerman was referring to—then realized that it was Blackburn.

"What do you mean?"

"He was talking to a couple of the other men up here by the counter," Hillerman said. "He said poker was one thing he knew he could beat you at. This fella seems to have a big grudge against you."

"It's nothing I'm encouraging, Jim," Pike said. "I got enough problems without making people mad at me— especially ones as young and big as Blackburn."

"He may be yonger," Hillerman said, "but my money goes on experience every time."

"I appreciate your support."

"Just keep an eye on him, Pike," Hillerman said. "From what I understand, this is his last chance to show you up. If he don't, he's gonna be pretty dangerous."

"I'll watch him."

"Pike!" McConnell called.

"Yeah?"

"Got some fellas here think a game of poker is a good

144

idea. You wanna sit in?"

Pike looked at Hillerman, who smiled and made a motion like a fisherman who had gotten a bite on his hook.

"Sounds like a good idea to me," Pike said, and walked over. . . .

They were about two hours into the game when the door opened and Blackburn entered with two other men Pike recognized as Tom Gary and Mike Collins. He wouldn't have thought so before, but the three of them seemed to be very chummy. They were also a little drunk, and Pike saw the almost empty whiskey bottle that Gary was holding down by his side.

He turned his attention back to his cards. They hadn't been kind for the first two hours, but they seemed to be coming his way now. He was holding two pairs, aces over fives, in a game of five card draw where all the players had already drawn cards.

The opener had been Matt Christopher, who now bet again.

Since they were betting against their shares of the sale of the skins when they got to St. Joe or St. Louis, in the beginning it had been up to McConnell to keep track of who was betting what. When that started to become confusing, Hillerman had solved the matter by supplying a batch of dried beans that they could use as chips. He had offered them kernels of corn, but the beans were bigger.

Christopher bet four beans. It was decided that each of the beans would represent two bits, so the game was not a particularly high stakes one.

Pat Lobro was next and he dropped out.

Joe Rand called the bet.

So did Paul Exman.

It fell to Pike now, and he decided to raise just once, to see how good a hand Christopher had. The man had opened, and had drawn three cards.

Pike raised four beans.

Christopher gave him a look across the table and called. The others dropped out.

"Aces over," Pike said.

"Beats me," Christopher said, and flipped over two kings to show his openers.

"You fellas got room for one more?" Blackburn asked.

The others didn't answer, but looked to Pike.

"Pull up a chair," Pike said. "It's just a friendly game."

Blackburn pulled a chair over and said, "They all started that way, don't they?"

Since Hillerman had not built his tables to accommodate poker games, they'd had to put two tables together. When Blackburn pulled his chair forward they had as many men around the two tables as was possible to have.

The game became more interesting after that.

CHAPTER SEVENTEEN

Pike had to give Blackburn his due, the man could play poker. It only took about fifteen minutes for everyone to realize that the game within the game was between Pike and Blackburn.

Everybody else was losing his beans.

Pike and Blackburn were involved in a hand when Pike looked up at McConnell and saw the tension on his friend's face. From where McConnell was sitting, he could only have seen Matt Christopher's hand, so the look had nothing to do with what Blackburn was holding. It probably had more to do with the fact that Blackburn had taken the last two hands.

They were playing seven card stud at the moment, with six cards in front of each of them. Blackburn was showing a pair of kings on the table, but he was betting like he had more, much more.

Pike had a pair of tens on the table, and he did have much more. The question was, did he have more than Blackburn did?

The others had dropped out and were watching the

action with great interest.

"Deal the last card," Blackburn said to Gary, smugly—too smugly. The last two hands he had been very sure that he was going to win, and he hadn't said a word the whole time. Also, his face had been expressionless. Now he was smug, and he was talking too much.

"Looks like these *beans* are finding themselves on my side of the table, huh?"

Pike didn't answer.

Blackburn picked up one of the beans on his side and stared at it, turning it this way and that.

"Yep, I might even have the old man cook these up for me for breakfast."

The last card fell in front of each of them and Pike waited to see how Blackburn would react. The black-bearded man picked the card up right away and looked at it.

That was when Pike knew he had him, and he looked at his own seventh card.

"Your bet," Tom Gary said to Blackburn.

"And I'm gonna do just that," Blackburn said. "I think I'm gonna bet . . . oh, how does twenty beans sound?"

Blackburn pushed the beans into the center of the table and grinned at Pike.

"It'd sound like a whole lot more if the beans were worth a dollar each instead of two bits," Pike said, after a moment.

"A dollar?" Blackburn said.

"That's right."

"You're sayin' you wanna raise the stakes?"

"That's what I'm saying."

Blackburn was stuck. To refuse to raise the stakes would make him look small in the eyes of the other men. He knew that. He also knew that his hand couldn't beat Pike's, or why would Pike be trying to raise the stakes.

Then he started to fool himself. Maybe Pike was just trying to scare him, trying to steal the pot.

Maybe Pike didn't really want to raise the stakes at all?

"All right," Blackburn said, "all right. The beans are worth a dollar each."

"And the bet stands?" Pike asked.

Blackburn looked around at the other men, then said, "No, the bet don't stand. I'll put in twenty more beans," and did so, emphatically. "Forty beans."

"Forty dollars," Pike said, just so everyone would understand.

"Right," Blackburn said, "forty dollars."

"All right, then," Pike said, looking down at his own pile of beans. "I'll call your forty beans, and bet sixty more."

Pike pushed that many beans into the center of the table while Blackburn watched. One of the other men sighed, and Pike could see the glitter in McConnell's eye. His friend knew that he had the winning hand.

"The bet's sixty—" Gary started, but Blackburn stopped him cold.

"I know what the damn bet is!" he snapped. He glared across the table accusingly at Pike and said, "You think you're gonna steal this pot, don't you?"

"I made my bet," Pike said, staring across the table at the younger man.

"Yeah, you made the bet," Blackburn said. He

looked down at what he had left in front of him and said, "I'm bettin' it all."

"John—" Tom Gary said. "Maybe you shouldn't—"

"Shut up!"

"Blackie—" Mike Collins said.

"All of it!" Blackburn said.

There was no way of knowing whether or not all of those beans represented Blackburn's total share of what they were going to sell, but it must have represented most of it.

"All right," Pike said, and pushed in what he had left. Nobody seemed to care to count the beans to make sure the bets were even. It was enough for everyone that they were both all in.

"What have you got?" Pike asked.

"Three kings," Blackburn said, and turned over the third king triumphantly.

"No good," Pike said, even before Blackburn could reach for the pot. He turned over his third ten, as well as a three that matched one on the table.

"Full house," Tom Gary said. "Pike wins."

Pike reached across the table and raked in all of the beans.

"Are we still playing?" Pike asked.

"Damn you," Blackburn said.

"Take it easy—" Pike said.

"Goddamn you—" Blackburn suddenly lunged across the table, but McConnell and Christopher were quicker. They each grabbed ahold of him and held him back.

"Let me go!"

"When you relax," McConnell said.

"You think you're so great," Blackburn said to Pike.

"You think you're so high and mighty. First you take Rita and *ruin* her for me—"

McConnell looked at Tom Gary and said, "You better take your friend out of here."

Gary nodded and looked at Mike Collins. McConnell and Gary lifted Blackburn from his chair. The black-bearded man didn't resist. When McConnell released his arm, Collins took it. He and Gary walked Blackburn to the door while the man was glaring at Pike over his shoulder.

"You'll get yours someday," Blackburn said to Pike. "You'll get it, Pike—"

Gary and Collins hustled Blackburn out the door, cutting him off.

"Gentlemen," McConnell said, "I think the game is over."

The others looked around at each other, then shrugged, rose, and left, leaving their beans on the table.

"Well?" Pike said to McConnell.

"Well what?"

"This game was your bright idea," Pike said. "What am I supposed to do with all these beans?"

"You gotta give 'em back to me," Hillerman said, coming over to the table. "I need them for tomorrow's dinner."

With that Hillerman swept all the beans from the table into a pot and walked away.

McConnell sat down across from Pike, gathered the cards and shuffled them.

"I guess it's a good thing we all left our rifles back in the camp, huh?" McConnell said. He was speaking about their temporary camp outside the settlement.

Pike had his Kentucky pistol in his belt, but had not felt the need to pull it. He agreed with McConnell. If Blackburn had had his rifle next to him, he might have gone for it.

"He really hates you, now," McConnell said.

Pike stared at McConnell.

"I know, I know," McConnell said, "the game was my idea."

Pike put his chin in his hand and looked at the ceiling.

"Want to play?" McConnell asked.

"No!"

McConnell shrugged and started dealing out solitaire.

"Uh," McConnell said, "you're not going to, uh, give them all back their beans . . . are you?"

CHAPTER EIGHTEEN

When Pike and McConnell left Hillerman's to turn in, Pike found Donna Lee waiting outside for him.

"I'll catch up to you, Skins," he said.

"No you won't," Donna said.

Pike looked at McConnell, shrugged, and said, "Maybe I won't."

"See you in the morning," McConnell said.

McConnell walked away and Pike turned to face Donna Lee.

"I was wondering where you disappeared to," Pike said.

"I didn't think you wanted me hanging around you," Donna said. "I thought I'd find a good place to camp away from the others."

Pike could understand that. She was a woman, and didn't necessarily want to bed down near a bunch of snoring mountain men.

"Did you find a place?"

"I sure did," she said, "and it's big enough for two."

He took that as an invitation, which was exactly how she intended it.

Donna had found a clearing well away from the settlement, and had set out her blanket and Pike's side by side. Pike noticed his horse picketed right next to hers, and his gear was laid out in camp. Everything was there, including his rifle. There was a fire going, and a pot of coffee on it.

"All the comforts of home," she said, as they sat around the fire.

She poured him a cup of coffee and handed it to him, then poured one for herself.

"What do you think?" she asked.

"About the coffee, the camp . . . or the company?" he asked.

"All three."

"They're fine."

She peered at him across the fire and cocked her head to one side.

"When's the last time you had a home?"

"Not for a long time," he said. "Not for any long period of time, anyway."

"Would you want one?" she asked. "I mean, I'm not tryin' to trap you or anythin'. I'm just makin' conversation."

"I understand."

He thought fleetingly about the cabin he had built where he and the Crow woman, Sun Rising, had lived until she was killed by five white men. That was the closest he had ever come to having a home. The pain of losing it was too much for him to want to repeat.

"So?"

"I like moving around too much," he said. "I wouldn't want to be tied down."

"That's honest enough."

"What about you?"

"Well, it's kind of hard to say."

"Why?"

"I've been sort of tied to this place for a long time," she said. "I'm lookin' to travel some, see places I ain't never seen before. I don't know how much of that will be enough, though."

"Once you start," he said, "it's hard to stop."

And when you do stop and put down some roots, he thought, somebody comes along and rips them up.

"I know what that's like." She stood up and came around to his side of the fire, sat next to him. "I feel that way, too . . . about some things."

She kissed him and he put his coffee cup down so he could take her in his arms.

They stripped off each other's clothes right there by the fire, oblivious—for the moment, anyway—to the chill in the air.

She kissed his shoulders and his chest, licking his nipples, sliding her hand down into his lap to take hold of him.

"The blankets . . ." she whispered. "It's cold . . ."

"I don't feel the cold," he said, sliding his hand over her belly. "I feel heat. . . ."

He slid one arm beneath her legs and lifted her up in his arms easily. He carried her to the blankets and laid her down gently.

"For a big man," she said, "you have very gentle hands." She took one of his hands in hers and brought it up to her lips. She kissed it, then ran her tongue over the fingers. Finally, she sucked his index finger into her mouth.

He ran his other hand over her body, starting with her legs and thighs, then over her belly, her ribs, until he was squeezing first one breast and then the other. Finally, he slid his hand between her legs and dipped one finger into her. She was wet, and steaming hot. She moaned, and her head lolled back as she bit her bottom lip.

He grabbed a third blanket, lay down beside her, and covered them both with it. They pressed together, kissing, legs intertwined, until finally he slid atop her, and then into her. She cried out and clutched him to her, lifting her knees high. He slid his hands beneath her buttocks and began to drive into her. She raked his back with her nails and cried out without fear of being heard because they were out in the middle of nowhere.

"Tell me what's goin' on," she said later, as they lay, still naked, huddled together beneath the blankets.

"What do you mean?"

"I mean there's more goin' on here than meets the eye," Donna said. "When do you intend to let everyone else in on it?"

"Well," he said, "I had intended to do it the morning that we left . . ."

"If you tell me," she said, "I won't tell the others. I'll leave that to you."

"All right," he said, and told her that they more than suspected that they were being watched, and had been being watched for many weeks, or even months.

"That can only mean one thing," she said. "Somebody's gonna try to rob us—I mean, you."

"You can say us," Pike said, "since I figure they'll try it once we're on the boats, and you'll be right there with us."

"I can shoot pretty good," she said, "so that's not a problem."

"Good."

"I don't have a rifle, though," she added. "That's a problem."

"That's not a problem," he said. "We'll get you one tomorrow."

"A new one?" she asked, snuggling closer. "I love presents."

"You don't have any money?" he asked.

"If I did," she said, "I'd buy my own gun."

"All right," he said, "I'll buy you a gun, but not a new one."

"Oh, all right."

They lay together for a while in silence, staring up at the sky, and then she asked, "Do you know who it is?"

"We have an idea," he said, and explained about Devers and the Frenchman.

"I've heard of Devers," she said. "He's a bad one, ain't he?"

"Yes," Pike said, "he's a bad one."

She looked at him, sensing something in the way he answered.

"He did somethin' to you, didn't he?"

"He killed a friend of mine."

"When?"

"Oh, it was a while back."

"But you ain't forgot, right?"

157

"That's right."

"You're hopin' it is him, don't you? You're hopin' he *does* try to rob us."

"Now why would I hope that?"

"Pike—"

"Go to sleep, Donna," he said. "Just go to sleep."

She started to argue, then thought better of it and went to sleep.

The next couple of days went slowly for Pike. He was eager to get going on the mackinaws, get the skins delivered, and get on with his life. Somewhere in between there, however, he knew he was going to have to deal with Cal Devers.

The second night they played poker again, but Blackburn didn't show up for the game. Pike made sure that the others knew that they were "just playin' for beans," and to pass the time. Everyone agreed that was best.

The night before they were to pick up the mackinaws Donna woke to find Pike sitting up, staring at the sky.

"What's wrong?" she asked.

"Nothing."

"You're just starin' at the sky for no good reason?" she asked.

He looked at her and said, "I've got a good reason."

"What is it?"

He waved his hand and said, "It's there."

"Pike," she said, "let's go to sleep. We've got to get up early and pick up those boats."

"I know," he said. "I know that."

She lay back down, leaving her hand on his lower

158

back. After a moment he felt it slide off, and knew that she had fallen asleep. He went to the fire and added some wood so it would keep going all night, then went back, slid into the blankets with her, and went to sleep himself.

In the morning Pike and Donna were the first ones at the boatyard. McConnell was next, with Lobro and Styles, and then the others started arriving.

Both mackinaws were on the river, tied to the dock, and the men—and Donna—stood there looking at them while Pike went inside to settle up.

When he reappeared, McConnell said, "All paid up?"

"All settled," Pike said. "They're ours."

"Let's go have a look," McConnell said.

They all walked out onto the docks to take a look at the boats, Blackburn taking up the rear.

Pike and McConnell boarded each boat to check them out, and pronounced them sound.

"More than sound," McConnell said. "They did some good work here."

"Let's get under way," Pike said. "With the way the river is flowing, we should be able to make camp by nightfall."

The mileage they would have to cover on the river was actually more than they had covered by land, but since they'd be moving much faster it wouldn't take as long to get back to camp.

"We'll have to tie the boats off and then load them in the morning," Pike said.

Pike took his crew onto his boat and got them settled

in with their oars. He looked over at McConnell's boat and saw that everyone was aboard but Blackburn. The big, black-bearded man was still standing on the dock.

"Come on, Blackburn," Pike heard McConnell say. "We got to get goin'."

"I'm comin', I'm comin'," Blackburn said, but he didn't move.

Pike was about to climb out of his boat onto the dock when McConnell saw him and waved him away. Pike subsided. It was only right, he guessed, that McConnell handle his own crew.

He watched as McConnell cajoled Blackburn onto the boat, and then set him up at the bow with his rifle, in his position on watch.

"Ready?" Pike called out to McConnell.

"We're ready," McConnell said, waving.

Pike untied the two lines holding his mackinaw to the dock and felt the current start to take the boat downriver. He eased past the oarsmen—three on each side—to his position as steersman. He turned and looked behind him and saw that McConnell's boat was moving smoothly behind them.

They were finally on the water.

CHAPTER NINETEEN

Pike felt at home on the river almost immediately. There was something about the smell of the water, and the sway of the boat beneath his feet, that he found very comforting. He'd never trade it in for riding a horse over a mountain, but he thought that the change once in a while would definitely be good.

He watched his six oarsmen carefully. Donna, the most experienced, seemed to be doing fine, while the others were unsure of themselves. After a while, though, they got into a rhythm and seemed to be doing all right.

He turned every so often to look behind them, just to make sure that McConnell's boat was still with them. Once, McConnell waved to him to let him know that everything was all right.

After a few hours on the river Pike decided to try bringing it to shore. He signaled to McConnell what he was going to try to do, and McConnell stayed right with him. They both steered the boats successfully to shore, but rather than keep them there they once again gave the boat up to the current, which kept them going at a lively pace.

Before leaving Fort Pierre Pike had made arrangements with Hillerman to put up his and McConnell's horses. The other men were left to make their own arrangements. Hillerman was told that if they didn't return for them in six months, they were his. Pike figured to get a new horse in St. Joe or St. Louis— they hadn't yet decided exactly what their destination would be. He doubted that he'd ride to Fort Pierre again specifically to pick up the horse he'd left there. Whatever gear was important to him had been stowed on the boat.

After a while Pike steered the boat almost without thinking about it. He watched the shore go by, and a couple of times thought he saw some Indians watching them, but just in passing.

He hoped that Harley Rose would set someone out to watch for them, because Pike wasn't all that sure he would recognize the place he and Rose had picked out to load the skins.

Every so often the oarsmen would rest and just leave the boat to the current. During one of these instances Donna left her position to join him.

"How do you like it?" she asked.

"I feel like I've been doing it all my life," he said.

"Would you want to spend the rest of your life on the water?" she asked.

He told her no, and explained how he felt, that an occasional trip downriver would not be a bad idea.

"Where are we headed—I mean, for you to sell your skins? St. Joe, or St. Lou?"

"We haven't decided yet," Pike said. "My vote would

162

be for the first we arrive at. That would be St. Joe. Some of the men might think that we'd get a better price in St. Louis, though. I guess we'll have to wait and see."

She turned and looked at the boat behind them. On the bow she could make out Blackburn's bushy black beard. She waved once, but he did not return it.

"Is it my imagination," Pike asked, "or is the current letting up some?"

"Seems to be," she said. "We'd better get back to the oars."

She returned to her position and the six oarsmen went back to work.

Every so often Matt Christopher would turn to face Pike and signal that he hadn't seen anything that suggested danger. The man turned now and Pike waved. He wasn't surprised. After all, this wasn't supposed to be the part of the trip that was dangerous.

Devers made sure that he was on watch on the fifth day. He wanted to be the first one to spot the mackinaws on the river. It was with great satisfaction that he did so, about an hour before it would have gotten dark.

"You made it, Pike," he said to himself, rubbing his hands together. "Now the fun starts."

Harley Rose set watches on the river starting with the fourth day. When the two mackinaws came into sight it was a man named Delbert Cole who saw them. As planned, he fired a shot to signal the camp, and then moved to the river's bank so he could wave the boats in.

Pike heard what he thought was a shot, and then saw a man standing on the riverbank. By the time he had steered the boat to shore, more men had arrived from camp. Matt Christopher tossed out a couple of lines, and the men pulled the mackinaw in close to shore, but not up onto the bank. They secured the lines to some trees, and while the current pulled insistently at the boat, it held fast.

They did the same to the second boat, and then the crews started to disembark.

"They're beautiful!" Harley Rose said to Pike, shaking his hand.

"I hope you've got something hot to eat," Pike said. "Riding the river is wet, cold work."

"We've got pots and pots of soup, Pike," Rose said, shaking hands with McConnell. "Glad to see all of you," he shouted happily.

Rose had not been kidding about the amount of soup that had been made. Huge pots of it sat in fires, presided over by Sheila and some of the other women. Pike sat with Rose and ate soup while he told the man about their trip.

"So our oarsmen worked out pretty good, huh?" Rose said.

"They were fine," Pike said, "but it was just a short hop from Fort Pierre to here. We'll have to see how they hold up during the long haul."

"How long a trip you figure it's gonna be?"

Pike shrugged and said, "It's got to be eight or nine hundred miles. With the current we have, we ought to be able to make that in eight or nine days."

"You think Donna can hold up that long?" Rose asked.

"Donna's the last one I'm worried about, Harley," Pike said.

"And Blackie?"

"You'll have to ask McConnell how Blackie did. He was on his boat."

Pike could see that Rose still had high hopes for John Blackburn. He hoped that "Blackie" would somehow turn over a new leaf and not disappoint the man who had so much faith in him.

Maybe Pike could even turn the leaf over for him—that is, if he could stand to get that close to him.

"Should we have someone watch the boats tonight?" Rose asked.

"I think that's a good idea, Harley," Pike said. "I don't think anyone's going to try anything with the boats, but the ropes could always come loose. Make sure whoever you put on watch knows enough to tug on those ropes from time to time."

"I'll set up a watch with three men. We'll want to start loading at first light."

"I want to get as early a start as possible," Pike said. "Let's use horses as well as mules to haul the skins down to the boat in the morning."

"Good idea."

"This soup was a good idea, too," Pike said. "I'm going to see if I can get another bowl."

He got up and walked to the nearest pot, which was

165

being watched by Sheila. McConnell was sitting with her, eating. When Pike approached, Sheila got up and left. She either wanted to leave them to talk alone, or just didn't want to be near Pike. She probably still held a grudge for the way she felt he had treated Rita.

"Harley was asking about Blackburn, Skins," Pike said while he ladled out some soup into his bowl. "That made me wonder, too. Just how did he handle the trip?"

"He stood at that bow the whole time, Pike, and never moved," McConnell said. "His shoulders were held high and tight, you know? Like you do when you're waiting for somethin' to hit you?"

"Is he going to be able to stay that way for eight or nine days?"

"I don't know," McConnell said. "When we all got off the boat he ran off and upchucked into some bushes. I guess we're just gonna have to wait and find out."

"Well," Pike said, sitting down next to his friend, "as long as he can shoot when the time comes."

"I wonder when that'll be?" McConnell said.

"I don't think they're going to let us get too far downriver before they hit up," Pike said. "Probably the first day."

"I hope so," McConnell said. "I'd like to get it over with quick so we don't have to be looking over our shoulders that whole time."

"Oh, we'll get it over with, all right," Pike said.

McConnell looked at his friend and wondered if Pike was just thinking about protecting the skins, or if he was figuring on taking care of Cal Devers once and for all.

CHAPTER TWENTY

The night went by without any alarms raised, and Pike thought he was the first one to rise until he smelled the coffee. Before getting himself a cup, however, he decided to walk down to the river to check on the boats himself.

When he reached the river he was surprised to see no one on watch. Harley Rose had assured him that he would have men on watch. Had whoever had the last watch decided that the arrival of first light was his signal that his shift was over? If he had, Pike was going to find out who he was and—

He looked down at the boats and noticed that one appeared to be drifting away. Even as he watched it moved further from shore. He took off on the run, hoping to reach it before it got too far away.

As he approached the water he saw both lines being dragged in the water. He splashed into the river and was up to his knees before he caught one of the lines. He grabbed the rope in both hands and pulled, but the current had caught the boat and was anxious to be off with it. He braced his legs and felt the muscles in his back as he strained to pull the boat back to shore. At best it was a standoff. He wasn't able to pull it in, and the current wasn't able to pull it away from him. He wasn't going to be able to hold it forever. He needed help, and the only way he was going to get some was to yell for it. He could have fired his Kentucky pistol, but that would have meant releasing the rope with one hand to reach it, and if he did that he was afraid he'd lose the mackinaw for good.

He started shouting "Help," over and over, hoping that someone would wake up and hear him. The rope began to slip in his hands because it was wet. He tried to wrap it around one of his arms, but was able to loop it only once, and even then he lost a couple of feet of it. The end of the rope was now dangling down between his legs.

He could feel the sweat under his arms and at the small of his back as he continued to yell. Just when he was afraid he was going to lose it he heard someone shouting behind him.

"Hold on! Hold on, Pike!"

It was McConnell. He came splashing into the water, moved ahead of Pike until the water was up to his waist, and grabbed the rope. Immediately, Pike felt the relief in his muscles, but he didn't let go. Together, they started pulling the boat to them, but the current was fighting them. Finally, another man splashed into the water, and a second, and they grabbed the other line. With four of them pulling both lines, they managed to fight the boat back toward shore and secure the lines again.

"Jesus," McConnell said, "how did that happen?"

"I don't know," Pike said. "Let's take a look."

The other two men who had helped were Lobro and Styles, and they were standing by, wet to the waist.

"Hey, you fellas try and find out who was supposed to be on watch this morning, and then find him."

"Right," Lobro said.

He and Styles went off to do what they were told, and Pike said, "Let's take a look at these ropes."

Pike looked at the end of one rope, while McConnell checked the other. When Pike picked up the end of the rope it was obvious that it had been cut.

"Whataya got?" McConnell called.

"It was cut."

"This one, too."

Pike walked over to McConnell and looked at his rope. The end was frayed, like it had been cut with a knife, same as the other one.

"Okay," he said, "that lookout may be lying around here somewhere. Let's take a look around."

They separated and started looking, and after a few moments McConnell called, "Pike!"

Pike hurried over to where McConnell was standing and saw the man lying on the ground behind some rocks.

"He's alive," McConnell said, crouching over the man, "but he's got a lump on the back of his head."

Pike heard someone approaching and looked up. It was Harley Rose and John Blackburn.

"What's goin' on?" Rose asked. "Pat Lobro said one of the boats got loose?"

"It didn't just *get* loose," Pike said. "Somebody cut the line."

"Why would—" Blackburn started, but Pike went on

without giving him a chance to finish.

"Harley, check the other lines and make sure that second boat doesn't break loose."

"All right—hey, is that Pete Fry?"

"He's all right," Pike said. "Somebody hit him over the head. Was he one of the men you put on watch?"

"Yeah," Rose said, "he had the third and last watch. Is he—"

"Better get those lines checked," Pike said. "If someone cut this one, they might have done the same to the other."

"We'll check it out," Rose said. "Come on, Blackie."

As they walked away Pike heard Blackburn saying, "Why do you let him talk to you like . . ."

"Let's get him up on his feet," Pike said of the man Rose had identified as Pete Fry.

They didn't get him to his feet, but they managed to get him to a seated position on the rocks.

"Pete? You know where you are?"

"Huh? Oh, yeah, sure. What happened?"

"That's what I want to ask you," Pike said. "What happened here? Who hit you?"

"Somebody hit me?" Fry asked, touching the back of his head. "Oh, yeah . . . hey, somebody hit me!"

"Good," Pike said, "now that we all agree, can you tell us who did it?"

"Uh"—the man frowned, thinking hard,—"no, no, I didn't see anyone. I just—all of a sudden everythin' just went . . . blank."

"Come on," Pike said, "think. Whoever hit you cut the lines of one of the mackinaws."

"*Both* mackinaws," Harley Rose said, coming up behind them.

170

"Both?" Pike said.

"The lines on the second boat were cut almost all the way through. A few more minutes and the pressure would have snapped them."

"Great."

"Blackie is tyin' them off again."

Pike turned to Fry again and said, "Think about it. What happened?"

"I was sittin' here, watchin' the boats. I . . . I guess I heard somethin' behind me—"

"You guess? You did, or you didn't?"

"All right," Fry said, "I heard somethin', but before I had a chance to turn around, somebody hit me."

Pike put his hand on the man's shoulder and said, "All right." He turned to Rose and said, "Why don't you have Blackie take Fry back to camp. Maybe they can put something on his head."

"Right."

Pike touched Rose's arm and said, "That is, if you don't mind."

Rose frowned and said, "Cut it out."

"What are we gonna do?" McConnell asked.

"Let's look around before the ground around here gets trampled. Maybe we'll find something."

"Like what?"

"I don't know," Pike said. "Footprints, maybe whoever hit Fry and cut the ropes dropped something."

"Why bother?" McConnell asked. "We already know who did it."

"Who?"

"Devers, or one of his gang."

"No," Pike said, hesitantly, "I don't think so."

"Why not?"

"There's no profit in it for Devers. He *wants* us on the water, away from camp, away from most of the men. This just doesn't pay for him."

"Maybe one of his gang thought it would be a good idea."

"Maybe, but I doubt that, too. I don't think any of Devers's men would do anything without his say-so. Come on, let's have that look around."

"What's happening?" Devers asked, looking up from his coffee at Sandy Dunlap. "You're supposed to be watching the camp. Are they loading yet?"

"No," Dunlap said, "they had a problem."

"What kind of problem?"

"Somebody cut the lines of their boats."

Devers gave the man a quick look.

"They lost their boats?"

"No," Dunlap said. "Pike got there in time to grab one as it was floating away. They got to the other one before the ropes snapped."

"Jesus!" Devers said, standing up quickly.

"What is wrong?" Henri LeConte asked, coming up from behind.

"I'll tell you what's wrong," Devers said. "Somebody almost ruined our plan, that's what."

"What do you—"

"Who cut the lines?" Devers asked Dunlap. "Did you see?"

"I saw a dark-haired woman. She sneaked up behind the watch, hit him over the head, and then cut the lines with a knife, only she didn't cut them all the way through. After she left, one of the boats broke free.

172

Pike came along and grabbed it before they could lose it."

"Well," Devers said, "thank God for Pike, huh?" He looked at LeConte and said, "Come on, let's go and have a look."

Pike and McConnell checked the area and didn't come up with anything that would tell them who cut the lines of the boat.

"What do we do now?" McConnell asked.

Pike looked out at the boats and said, "I guess we forget about it."

"Just forget about it?"

"Let's just get the boats loaded and get under way," Pike said. "That's what we really need to do, isn't it, Skins?"

"I guess so," McConnell said, "but how do we find out who cut the lines?"

"We can leave that to Harley, after we're gone," Pike said. "Or maybe we'll never know."

"I don't like the idea of not knowing," McConnell said. "It could be one of our crew."

"It could be," Pike said. "I guess you and I will just have to keep our eyes on everyone, huh?"

It took the better part of the morning, and into the afternoon to load the almost five thousand skins they had, even with the use of horses as well as mules, but finally they were ready to go.

"While you're gone," Harley Rose said, "I'll try to find out who cut the boats loose."

"It doesn't really matter to me," Pike said. "I won't ever be seeing most of these people after this is all over—but for your own benefit—"

"I'll look into it," Rose said. "If it was one of my people, I want to know about it."

"I don't blame you."

The skins and pelts were on board, and so were the rest of the crew. McConnell had boarded his boat, and was waiting for Blackburn.

"Come on, Blackburn," he called out, "we don't have all day."

Rose started toward Blackburn, but Pike put his hand on his arm.

"Let me."

Pike walked over to Blackburn and said, "If there's a problem, Blackburn, let us know now, so we can replace you."

Blackburn turned to face Pike. The trepidation he was feeling turned to anger.

"You won't have to replace me," Blackburn said.

"Then get on the boat, and let's get going."

Blackburn's hand tightened on his gun. He turned quickly and got aboard McConnell's boat. McConnell tipped his chin to Pike in thanks.

Pike walked back to his own mackinaw and stepped aboard.

"Let 'em loose," Pike said to Rose. "Time to get these skins to market.

CHAPTER TWENTY-ONE

By the time Devers and LeConte returned to camp the other men had broken camp, and were ready to leave. As ordered, Sandy Dunlap, a couple of the other men, and a couple of the Indians had been sent on ahead to keep track of Pike's progress on the river.

"Is this going to work?" LeConte wondered out loud. "I mean, it's a lot of ground for us to cover—"

"Look," Devers said, "we have to assume that they know they're being watched. That means they'll expect to be hit the first day."

"I still don't understand—"

"It's simple, Henri," Devers said. "Pike will assume that we don't want to travel a long way before making our play for him. "We're gonna make him wait."

"What will that accomplish?"

"It'll make him and his people jumpy," Devers explained, impatiently, "and it just might make some of them think that he's wrong. If that happens, their guard will be down by the time we do hit."

"Devers—"

"Henri, I don't have time to try and convince you all over again," Devers said. "Don't I usually know what I'm doing?"

"Well . . . yes," LeConte said, "you do—"

"Then trust me now," Devers said. "Get the rest of the men and the other savages ready to go. We're leavin' in five minutes."

Just before they all boarded their mackinaws Pike explained to both crews what was happening, and what conclusions he had come to.

"Let's get this straight," Lobro said. "You think Cal Devers is gonna try to rob us?"

"That's right."

"While we're on the river?"

"Well, either that or when we come into shore at night. He knows we can't stay on the water forever."

"What do you want from us?" Lobro asked.

"Now's the chance for anyone who wants to quit to do it."

Lobro looked around, then said, "I don't think anyone wants to quit, Pike. After all, we worked hard for these skins."

"All right," Pike said. "That's what I thought everyone's answer would be, but I wanted to give you all a chance."

Now they were under way, and it was definitely too late for anyone to quit.

The mackinaws were moving along smoothly and swiftly, so Pike allowed the oarsmen to lift their oars for a while and enjoy the ride. Donna Lee left her position and joined him.

"So what do you think?" she asked.

"About what?"

"Who tried to cut the boats loose?"

"I don't know. Somebody who didn't want us to leave, I guess."

"And who didn't want you to leave?"

"I didn't think anyone wanted to keep us there. After all, everyone's livelihood depends on us getting our cargo delivered."

"Everyone?"

"Sure."

"I don't think so."

He looked at her and asked, "What are you talking about?"

"There was someone in camp who didn't want you to leave."

"Who?"

"Think about it?"

"Donna, I can't—wait a minute," he said, as something occurred to him. "You don't think it was Rita?"

"Who else wouldn't want you to leave?"

"But . . . she's not interested in me anymore, not since you came to camp."

"For a man who thinks he knows women, Pike," she said, "you don't know much about women, do you?"

"Donna—"

"When a woman says she's not interested, it means she is."

"But since you came—"

"So she's angry, and jealous. That doesn't mean she doesn't . . . want you."

"So she'd attack a man and cut the boats loose to

177

keep me there a little longer?"

"Sure, why not?"

"I don't buy it."

She shrugged and said, "Hey, it's just a theory. If you don't agree, that's fine."

They watched the landscape go by for a while and then she said, "Have you decided yet where you're taking the skins?"

"St. Louis," he said. "I talked to Harley and some of the others last night. They felt we'd get a better price there."

"And you?"

"I wanted to stop at St. Joe."

"Why?"

"I've been to St. Louis, and didn't like it," he said. "Also, I wanted to get this trip over as soon as possible."

"I guess you're not real happy with the way things have gone."

"I guess Skins and I should have kept on going that day in February, when we first rode into camp," he said. "That was my intention, anyway."

"What changed your mind?"

"Well, Sheila changed his mind," Pike said. "I'm not real sure what changed mine, but it's too late to cry about it now."

"You don't strike me as the kind of man who cries about much."

"Not usually."

Pike *didn't* usually complain, but he'd learned a lesson from this fiasco. From now on he'd stay on his own, or with Skins or whoever he was partnered with, but he was going to stay away from large hunting

178

camps. Putting that many people together caused nothing but trouble—and when you had women around, it was even worse.

Back in camp Harley Rose started asking questions. He couldn't believe that any of his people would deliberately cut the lines on the boats. He couldn't imagine who would have a motive to do such a thing.

He was sitting in front of his tent, having his dinner, when Rita came over to him.

"Can I talk to you?"

She seemed nervous, fidgeting from foot to foot and keeping her hands clasped in front of her.

"Sure," Rose said. "What about?"

"I have a confession to make."

"About what?"

"I'm the one who cut the lines on the boats this morning."

"What?" He looked up at her in disbelief. "Rita, why would you do such a thing?"

"I . . . wanted to keep Pike from leaving."

Rose stood up, becoming incensed.

"You did that on some . . . some fool romantic whim?" he shouted.

"Harley, I—"

"Rita, I can't believe you would be so . . . so stupid, so selfish. Getting those skins sold means too much to all of us for you to try to . . . to . . ." He was sputtering, unsure of what he wanted to say. "You could have killed Fry!"

"I know," she said. "I'm sorry. I didn't mean to hit him so hard."

179

"Well, you can tell him that."

"Tell him?" she said, alarmed. "You mean you want me to—"

"I want you to confess to everyone, just as you did to me, and apologize."

She looked down at the ground and said, "I suppose I should."

"And Pike," Rose said, "you should apologize to Pike, although I doubt you'll ever see *him* again."

"I know that."

"Go on," he said, "find Fry and start with him."

She nodded, biting her lip, and then said, "All right. I will."

As Rita walked away Harley Rose actually heaved a big sigh of relief. As angry as he had been at Rita for what she had done, at least he knew that no one in his camp had maliciously cut the ropes and tried to sabotage their attempt to get them to market.

Now all Pike and the others had to worry about was whether or not Cal Devers really was going to try and rob them.

CHAPTER TWENTY-TWO

Pike turned around to look at the second mackinaw and saw McConnell waving madly. When Pike gave McConnell all his attention the other man started pointing to shore. Pike looked and saw what his friend was pointing at. On the shore, keeping pace with them on horseback, were about three Indians.

Donna and the other men noticed Pike looking to shore and lifted their oars so they could look, as well.

Donna turned and looked at Pike.

"What do you think?" she asked.

"They might be Crow," he said, still peering in to shore. The Indians were urging their ponies on to keep pace with the mackinaws.

"What do you think they want?"

"They want us," Pat Lobro answered before Pike could.

"Us," Donna asked, "or our goods?"

"Both," Pike said, "or whichever they can get."

"Look," Pete Styles shouted, pointing ahead of them.

Pike looked and saw that they were approaching a bend in the river—a bend that would take them away from the Indians.

"Let's get on those oars," Pike said.

"They're gonna shoot at us!" Donna shouted.

"They don't have any rifles," Pike said. "Just keep alert."

No sooner had he spoken than an arrow landed very close to him, burying itself in the wooden floor of the boat. Several more fell, but landed harmlessly on the roof of the boat. Pike sneaked a look behind him and saw that the Indians were now aiming their arrows at McConnell's boat. He saw John Blackburn turn and fire his rifle, but by then they were both in the bend of the river, and out of harm's way.

They rode the steep bend in the river all the way around, and then Pike turned and saw McConnell signaling to make for shore.

Pike steered his boat close to shore, and Matt Christopher hopped down and ran to shore with a line to tie them off. When that line was tied, Pike jumped down and walked a second line to shore, securing it to a tree. Satisfied that his boat wasn't going anywhere, he turned and waded out to accept a thrown line from McConnell's boat. He tied that one off, and watched Christopher tie a second line.

Pike then approached McConnell's boat, and saw that someone had an arrow sticking out of him. He only hoped that it wasn't a fatal wound.

"Skins," he shouted, "who got hit?"

"Mike Collins took an arrow in the upper thigh," McConnell said.

Pike reached up and grabbed McConnell's hand, and was assisted into the boat. They both went over to where Mike Collins was sitting.

"How bad is it, Mike?" Pike asked.

"Damn thing's buried deep," Collins said. Pike could see the pasty white color of the man's skin, and the sweat that was pouring off of him.

"Stretch him out, and cover him with a blanket," Pike said.

They lifted Collins from his position and laid him down beneath the roof of the boat. As they covered him with a blanket Pike walked to the front of the boat and waved to his.

"Donna?" he called, and waved that she should come over. When she dropped into the water he waited for her to reach him, then reached down and pulled her aboard.

"What's wrong?"

"We've got an injured man," Pike said. "How good a nurse are you?"

"Let's take a look," she said.

"Move away," Pike told the other men who were crowded around their colleague.

There was room under the roof for Pike, Donna, and McConnell to crouch around the injured Mike Collins.

Collins was covered with a blanket, so they uncovered his left thigh. Pike took out his knife and cut away the man's pants. The arrow was buried deep into his thigh.

"That's gotta come out before we can do anything," Donna said. "We'll even have to dig it out, or push it through."

Mike Collins was a tall, slender man. He did not have the tree trunk thighs that Pike or John Blackburn had.

"Which way?" McConnell asked. "Out, or through?"

"Jesus," Mike Collins said, "push the damned thing through."

Pike and McConnell looked at each other and nodded.

"I'll hold him down," McConnell said.

"Get Blackburn to help," Pike said, asking for the biggest man on the boat.

Blackburn came over, looking a little green in the face. He knelt on the other side of Mike Collins and he and McConnell braced the man, rolling him over so that his thigh was off the floor of the boat.

Pike put one hand around the shaft of the arrow, and in one convulsive move, he drove the arrow through Collins's thigh, and out the other side. Collins cried out, his entire body tensing like the string of the bow that had fired the arrow into his thigh. That done, Pike reached beneath Collins and snapped the arrowhead off. That enabled him to pull the shaft back out through the entry wound.

Donna had already had some of the men tearing strips from their shirts, and now she said, "Let me get in there, Pike."

Pike moved aside to let Donna crouch next to Collins, who was now not being held by McConnell and Blackburn, but supported.

"I need some whiskey," Donna said.

"Whiskey?" Pike said. "We don't have any whiskey."

"Pike," she said, impatiently, "we have eleven men

184

on two boats. You mean to tell me not one of them sneaked some whiskey along?"

Pike stepped out from under the roof and faced the men on the boat.

"Who brought some whiskey along?"

Exman, Dennis, and Gary all exchanged glances, but none of them stepped forward.

"Look," he told them, "go to the other boat and see if anyone has a bottle of whiskey. We need it for the wound. I'm not going to ask who had it, I just want it— in the next two minutes."

"Make that one," Donna said. "I've gotta disinfect this wound and bind it before he gets infected."

"You heard the lady," Pike said. "Get moving."

"Hold it," Tom Gary said. "Never mind. I've got a bottle of whiskey along."

"Give it to me."

Gary went over to his gear, came out with a full bottle of whiskey and handed it to Pike.

Pike pulled the cork from the bottle and handed it to Donna. She in turn simply upended it onto Collins's wound. He cried out and strained against McConnell and Blackburn. She poured some whiskey onto a piece of cloth and pressed to the exit wound.

"Hold this," she told Pike. He leaned in with his arm, since there was no room for him, and pressed his hand to the cloth. Donna drenched another cloth and pressed it to the entry wound, then started to wrap the leg. Pike moved his hand out of the way, and she used all the cloth they had to bind the wound tightly enough to stop the bleeding.

"All right," she said, "let him rest."

185

McConnell and Blackburn eased Collins down to the deck and Donna covered him with the blanket again.

"Get something to put under his head," she said, moving out from beneath the roof and standing up. "Make him comfortable. He's not to move, or the bleeding will start again."

"I can row," Collins said, his voice faint.

"I know you can, Mike," McConnell said, "but you rest awhile, first."

McConnell and Blackburn came out from under the roof and faced Pike.

"We'll camp here for the night," Pike said. "In the morning we'll start off again." He turned to Blackburn and said, "You'll take Collins's position until he's well enough to row."

"All right," Blackburn said, meekly.

Pike was surprised at his reaction until he realized that rowing would put him in a seated position, which the big man would probably prefer to standing on the bow.

"We'll make camp on shore, but let's keep Collins here," Pike said to McConnell. "Let's get some extra blankets so he stays warm."

"All right."

"Donna," he said, "how about some coffee? We can get that in him."

"Give him some of the whiskey, too," she said.

"Right," Pike said, and then looked at the others and said, "but only him. I don't want anyone else drinking. Is that understood?"

They all nodded.

"I'm going over to my boat to tell the others," he said. "Why don't you fellas start moving some gear to shore and start collecting the makings of a fire."

"I'll stay with Collins," Donna said.

"Good idea."

"Yeah," McConnell said, grinning, "put his head in your lap. That would make *me* more comfortable."

CHAPTER TWENTY-THREE

They built one fire on shore, and set up two watches, one on the outskirts of the camp, and one on the boat, with Collins and Donna. Pike made the coffee, because Donna had stayed aboard the mackinaw with Collins. When it was ready he brought a cup out to each of them.

"Thanks, Pike," Donna said. She set her cup aside, lifted Collins's head, and gave him some.

"Thanks."

Pike sat on the end of the boat, dangling his feet over the edge. He had removed his shoes and socks, and rolled up his pants. The air was turning his feet to ice.

"Do you think those Indians were there by coincidence, Pike?" she asked.

"I don't know," he said. "There was only three of them, not big enough for a hunting party of any kind."

"Do you think they could be working with that man, Devers?"

"Who can tell?" Pike said. "It would depend on what he offered them."

"What would it take?"

He shrugged and said, "Beads, blankets . . . some whiskey? What we do know is that it wasn't Devers's main attack."

"You said he'd attack us on the first day."

"I said I thought he would attack on the first day," Pike said, correcting her. He stared down into the water. "Obviously, he's going to make us wait. He's willing to travel much further than I thought he would be."

"That doesn't disappoint you, does it?"

He looked at her and asked, "Now why do you say that, Donna?"

"Because now you know he's on your hook," she said, "and you can just bring him in whenever you want."

"Well, not whenever I want," Pike said, "but he's out there, maybe watching, certainly waiting." He looked at her and said, "What makes you so smart?"

"I think like a man."

He gave her a look.

"No, it's true," she said.

"If I told you that, you'd take it as an insult."

"Maybe," she said, "but it's true. I think like a man, which is why I can fit in. It's also the reason I don't have to fight men off."

"You don't fight them off?"

"I don't *have* to fight them off," she said. "I'm like one of the guys."

"You don't look like any guy I ever knew."

Donna looked down at Collins, who was either asleep or unconscious, then back at Pike with a different look on her face.

"Do you think if we went to the other boat and spent the night there the others would know what we were doin'?" she asked.

"How could they?" he asked, dropping down into the water to return to shore, "you're just one of the guys, remember?"

"Tell me," Devers said, looking at Henri LeConte and Sandy Dunlap.

"Three of our braves saw the boats this afternoon," LeConte said.

Devers waited, listening to the campfire crackle, then had to ask, "And?"

LeConte looked at Dunlap, who looked away.

"They fired on the boats."

"What?" Devers said. "Did they have rifles?"

"No, bows and arrows."

"Did they get anyone?"

"They said they thought they might have wounded one man."

"Damn!" Devers said. "Henri, I thought you said you could control these savages."

"They just didn't understand what we wanted from them, Cal," LeConte said.

"Well, do they understand now?" Devers demanded.

"Sure, Cal," LeConte said, "they understand. They're just to watch."

"They better understand," Devers said, "because I don't want anything else messing up our timetable, Henri. Understand?"

"Of course I understand," LeConte said. "I am not stupid, Cal."

Devers looked up at his partner, then decided not to say what was on his mind.

"All right," he said, "have some coffee and relax. Dunlap, set three watches—and don't give the Indians any of them."

"Right."

"Jesus," Devers said, rubbing his forehead, "what a bunch of dummies."

Pike did not have any of the watches. The luxury of command, he thought, but he couldn't sleep, anyway, so he was awake, sitting by the fire, with a cup of coffee in his hand.

Even if the Indians *were* working for Devers, Pike was sure that their little attack on the boats was not Devers's idea. In fact, when Devers found out about it, he was probably going to be very angry. If anything, the Indians were probably just supposed to keep the boats in sight, so that Devers could find them when he wanted them.

Pike looked out at the mackinaws, bobbing slightly as they fought to move with the current. Even though there were watches set, he decided to go and have a look at the lines. He was checking the ropes on the second boat when he came across Pat Lobro, his rifle held in the crook of his arm.

"You move quiet," Pike said.

"A habit I got into early," Lobro said. "Fella my size can usually move around quietly, and go unnoticed."

"I see what you mean," Pike said. "If there's anything I can't go, it's unnoticed."

"Yeah," Lobro said, "I'm sure being as tall as you are

can be a great disadvantage. How do the lines look?"

"Secure."

"Good," Lobro said, "they were secure when I checked them ten minutes ago, too."

"Oh, well . . ." Pike said, not wanting to insult the man since he *was* on watch, "I just couldn't sleep, so I thought I'd—I mean, it's not that I don't think you're capable—"

"Forget it, Pike," Lobro said. "Check 'em all you want. It can't hurt to double-check."

"Who else is on watch now?"

"Styles has the other side of the camp. Joe Rand is on one boat, and Blackburn's on the other one, with Donna and Collins."

"Okay," Pike said. "I guess I'll try and get some sleep."

"Good idea, Pike," Lobro said. "See you in the morning."

"Yeah, sure," Pike said.

Pat Lobro melted away into the darkness and Pike turned and walked back to the fire. When he got there he found Skins McConnell sitting with a cup of coffee warming his hands.

"You couldn't sleep, either?" Pike asked, sitting next to him.

"No," McConnell said. "I don't know what it is. Maybe it just feels funny having the ground under my feet after a whole day on the river. I thought I'd go and check the lines—"

"I checked them," Pike said, "about ten minutes after Lobro checked them. They're fine."

"Ooh," McConnell said, "did the little fella take offense?"

193

"Cut out that little fella stuff," Pike said. "Lobro's a good man."

Pike sat down and poured himself another cup of coffee. Around them they could hear the other men snoring, some loudly, some softly.

"You ever get the feeling that we made a mistake stayin' here?" McConnell asked.

Pike turned his head slowly and stared at his friend for a long moment.

"What?" McConnell said, staring back at his friend wide-eyed. "Oh, wait a minute, you're gonna blame me that we stayed, aren't you—"

"If you were thinking with your head instead of your beanie—"

"What? Wait a minute, Pike," McConnell said. "Are you sayin' that the only reason I wanted to stay was because of Sheila?"

Pike stared at him and said, "Give it a little thought, Skins."

"Pike . . ." McConnell said, shaking his head, "that's . . . that's just not . . . uh, it's . . . it's true, isn't it?"

"Yep."

McConnell stared out at the water like he was in some kind of stupor.

"Jesus," he said, "my head's been on crooked for months."

"Not crooked," Pike said, "it's just hard to think with it when it's between somebody's legs."

CHAPTER TWENTY-FOUR

Early the next morning Pike went out to McConnell's mackinaw to check on Collins's condition. He brought with him two cups of coffee.

"Good morning," he said, handing the two cups up to Donna. "How's the patient?"

"He ran a fever during the night," she said, " but it's gone down now."

Pike climbed aboard the boat.

"Is he going to be able to row?"

"Yes," Collins said from his position beneath the roof of the boat.

"Not today," Donna said, handing a cup of hot coffee to Collins. "Drink that."

From the boat Pike could see the men on shore breaking camp. Behind them he could see higher ground, and his eyes raked over it, looking for any sign of danger.

"We'll be moving in about twenty minutes," Pike said. "Donna, you'll row with this boat, so you can keep an eye on Collins. I'll be taking Paul Exman."

"All right."

"Blackburn will be replacing Collins."

"You stick me up on the bow with a rifle and I can keep watch," Collins said.

"You'll stay where you are, Mike. We'll see about you moving to the bow in a couple of days."

Collins nodded, and sipped his coffee.

"Drink up, people," Pike said. "We've got some time to make up."

They moved along at a lively pace for the better part of the morning, and then suddenly the river began to narrow. Pike didn't think anything of it, but when it continued to narrow he suddenly got an uncomfortable feeling. He turned and waved at McConnell until his friend saw him, and then signaled that they should move into shore.

When both boats were secured Pike waded out to McConnell's.

"What's wrong?"

"Have you noticed the way the river is narrowing?" Pike asked.

"Well, yeah, I did notice. So what?"

"So . . . what if it gets extremely narrow further up ahead."

"You mean so narrow that we won't be able to get through?"

"No," Pike said, "I mean so narrow that it would make a perfect place for an ambush."

"Oh, I see what you mean. What do you want to do about it?"

"I suggest you and I go on foot and take a look ahead," Pike said. "Everyone else can wait here."

"I'm with you," McConnell said.

"Just let me get my rifle."

As Pike started away Donna called out, "Pike?"

"Yeah?"

She leaned over the side to look at him and said, "Be careful, huh?"

He smiled and said, "Always."

Pike retrieved his rifle from his boat and gave instructions to Pat Lobro.

"Stay here and wait for us, Pat. We should be back within the hour."

"And if you're not?"

"You're going to have to decide that for yourselves," Pike said. "If we're not back, it's because something happened to us."

"I understand. Good luck."

Pike met McConnell on shore and said, "Come on. We'll have to set a fast pace. I told Lobro only to give us an hour."

"And if we don't find anything in that time?" McConnell asked.

"Then hopefully they'll be nothing to find."

They set off, not running full out, but trotting, keeping up a constant pace.

It was Pike's thought that if the river was going to narrow dangerously—to a point where an ambush was likely—it would happen very soon. When the ground started to rise steeply, he knew he was right. Before long they were high above the river, looking straight down. On both sides of the river it was straïght up and

197

down, and below the river narrowed considerably.

"If they're going to ambush us, they'd have to do it from up here," McConnell said, looking straight down. "There's no way they can get closer."

"I agree."

"And they'd have to be very good shots."

"They could roll some of these rocks down on us," Pike said, "but the current looks pretty quick down there. Even with the biggest boulders their aim would have to be perfect."

"Besides that," McConnell said, "I don't see anyone around here. If they're gonna ambush us here, where are they?"

"This might be one of the times I'm glad I'm wrong," Pike said. "Come on, let's get back to the others."

On the way back they discussed the current they had seen in the gorge.

"It looks three times as fast as what we've encountered so far," McConnell said, "and it looks rough."

"It probably is. The water probably picks up speed the narrower the gorge gets, the way air does. The boats are sturdy enough to make it, though."

"I know the boats are," McConnell said, "but are we? After all, we don't have the most experienced crews."

"What choice have we got, Skins?" Pike asked. "We've got to make do with what we've got."

"I just hope it's good enough."

When they got back they told everyone to gather on shore, except for Donna and Collins.

"Don't I get to find out what's happening?" Donna asked.

"Sure you do," Pike said. "You're one of the boys, remember?"

She stuck her tongue out at him.

"I'll tell you exactly what's going on myself, as soon as I finish with the others."

"I'll be waiting."

He waded back to the shore, where McConnell was waiting with the others.

"Okay," Pete Styles said, "so what's going on?"

Pike explained what they had seen ahead. No ambush, but a pretty rough ride through the gorge.

"And that doesn't mean there *won't* be an ambush when we get there," Pike added, "but having seen the area myself, it's not the spot I would pick."

"Why not?" Lobro asked. "I mean, if we're going to be occupied anyway, why not?"

"Because Devers doesn't want to sink us, that's why," Pike said. "He doesn't want the skins on the bottom of the river, and if he distracts us while we're going through that gorge, that's where they're going to end up."

"Makes sense," Joe Rand said.

"We'll go ahead and be ready for the gorge," Pike said. "But, Matt, you're going to have to keep a sharp eye out. If there's trouble, you're going to have to handle it."

"With one shot?" Matt Christopher asked. "I've never tried to reload while riding a mackinaw on the river, never mind through the raging gorge."

"We'll all supply you with our rifles," Pike said.

"You'll have six shots. If you have to use them, make them count."

"Don't worry," Matt Christopher said, "I will."

They all waded back out to their boats, and Pike took the time to fill Donna in.

"Sounds like we're in for a fun ride," she said.

"Let's hope that's all we're in for," Pike replied.

CHAPTER TWENTY-FIVE

Before starting downriver again they decided to lash anything that was loose to the deck, so that they wouldn't lose any supplies overboard. That included Mike Collins. Once that was done, they released their lines and gave themselves up to the current.

Another thing Pike came up with was the suggestion that when they reached that gorge, they should pull in their oars, lest they be snapped off. They were going to have to rely on the current, and their steersmen—Pike and McConnell—to get them through.

The river continued to narrow on them, and then the ground around them began to slope upward. Before long, the ground was almost sheer on both sides, and suddenly the current was growing stronger.

"Here we go!" Pike shouted. "Haul those oars in!"

The oarsmen did as they were told. They pulled in the oars, and then took hold of anything they could and braced themselves for the ride.

Suddenly, the river began spouting water up onto

them. It hit the decks in great gouts, but the builders had prepared for that, and there were drain-off holes in the deck. Still, the water seemed to almost fill the boats, and several of the men were afraid that they were going to be flooded, or capsized, and sunk.

John Blackburn vomited on himself so many times that he mercifully lost consciousness.

Some of the other men wished they could do the same.

It was all Pike could do to hold onto the tiller, and he hoped McConnell was able to hang on. His friend had neither *his* size nor his bulk, and he was having difficulty. He hoped that McConnell would ask for help if he needed it.

Now they were being buffeted about and the water around seemed to have turned white. There were waves, as if they were on the sea instead of a river, and the boat—in spite of all Pike's efforts—began to spiral, being turned round and round by the current as it was carried through the gorge.

Pike knew that they were in bad trouble if either boat struck the wall. The builders had done the best they could, but by their very nature mackinaws were not the sturdiest of crafts. If they struck the wall, they'd splinter for sure, and everything would go to the bottom—boat, skins, and people.

Pike couldn't see McConnell's boat because of the swells in the water. When Pike's boat was up, McConnell's was down, and vice versa. It was hopeless to try and keep track of his friend's boat.

At one point they began to spin so fast that Pike was afraid they were caught in a whirlpool of some kind. He leaned into the tiller and was amazingly able to straighten the boat out and keep it straight. It was then that he realized that the current was letting up.

They had made it through the worst part.

The current was still deadly, and there was still the danger of slamming into a wall, but it began to let up more and more noticeably, and then suddenly the sheer walls on both sides fell away, and the water grew calmer. . . .

Everyone was so stunned by the ride that it took them a few moments to realize that they had made it, and then they all started to cheer. They even stood up from their positions and pounded Pike on the back for having successfully taken them through the gorge. Pike decided to take the praise and not let them know that he had little or nothing to do with it.

Pike turned to look behind them and the pit of his stomach turned cold.

He couldn't see McConnell's boat.

The others became aware that the other boat wasn't behind them and grew suddenly quiet.

Had the gorge taken their friends—and half their goods—to the bottom of the river? They all searched in vain for any sign of the boat, even debris, but there was none . . . and then suddenly there it was, and the wild cheering began anew.

They had all made it through in one piece.

"All right, all right!" Pike shouted above the din. "Let's check for damages."

He looked at the deck and saw that all of the water they had taken on had drained off. As long as the structure of the boat was sound they wouldn't even have to stop. That is, unless they were waved to stop by McConnell.

McConnell had had one very bad moment in the gorge when his boat had actually scraped against one of the sheer walls. He'd heard something crack, but the boat seemed to handle the impact fairly well. Now that they were out of the gorge he shouted for everyone to check the boat for damages.

Up ahead he saw Pike's boat, and he and his crew were waving their arms. They seemed to be cheering, and he waved back.

He knew Pike would be checking for damage to his boat as well. If both had come through unscathed, they could simply continue in their way.

That was not to be the case, however.

"Skins!" Donna shouted.

"What?"

She came up to him, her short dark hair plastered to her head.

"We've got a crack in the hull."

"Damn!"

That was the crack they had all heard when they hit the wall.

"Are we takin' in water?"

"Can't tell," she said. "We're gonna have to stop and take a better look."

"All right," he said. "We better wave Pike down. Have Blackburn do it."

"Uh, Blackburn is unconscious."

"Did he get hurt?"

204

"No," she said. "I, uh, think he fainted."

"Oh, great . . ." McConnell said.

Pike looked back and saw Donna waving to him, and then pointing to shore.

"Something's wrong," he called to the others. "We're going to have to stop."

"Our boat's okay," Lobro said. "No damage that we can see."

"They must have some damage," Pike said, "and we're going to have to see if we can fix it."

Lobro looked at Pike and said, "Can you repair a mackinaw?"

"I don't know," Pike said. "I've never tried."

Once they had the boats secured, Pike and McConnell got into the water to inspect the damage done to McConnell's boat.

"It's a crack, all right," Pike said.

"I can see that," McConnell said. "How bad a crack is it?"

"I don't know," Pike said. He touched it and said, "One thing is for sure. If we don't fix it, it's going to get bigger."

"And how do we fix it?" McConnell asked.

"What are you asking me for?" Pike said. "Come on, let's get back to the others."

When they returned to shore Donna asked, "How bad is it?"

"It's a crack," McConnell said.

"I *know* that," she said. "How *bad* is it?"

"We don't know," McConnell said.

"But we're going to have to fix it," Pike said. "If we don't, it's going to get bigger."

"So who knows how to fix it?" Pat Lobro asked.

"Not me," McConnell said.

"Not me, either," Pike said. "Anybody else? Rand? Pat, you don't know?"

"Not me," Lobro said, and Rand and the others all shook their heads.

"Anybody want to ask me?" Donna asked.

Pike looked at her in surprise and said, *"You* know how to fix it?"

"Well," she said, "I won't know that until I look at it, but I know one thing for sure."

"What's that?"

"I know a damned sight more about it than any of you jokers."

And with that she waded out to the mackinaw to have a look.

"You think she really knows how to fix it?" McConnell asked.

"I hope so," Pike said, "or we're going to be here awhile."

They waited impatiently for her to come back, and when she did Pike said, "Well?"

"It's bad," she said.

"Will it hold?" McConnell asked.

She shook her head.

"I think we'd be taking in water before long."

"Enough to sink her?" McConnell asked.

"That and more."

206

"Can we fix it?" he asked.

"Sure we could fix it," she said. "The damage is only to one board. We could fix it *if* we had a replacement board, *and* some nails, and a hammer. All we need is the right equipment."

"You mean we can't fix it?" McConnell asked.

"Does anybody have a hammer on them?" she asked.

Nobody answered.

CHAPTER TWENTY-SIX

"Wait a minute," Pike said, some time later.

They had built a fire and put on a big pot of coffee. They were all sitting on the ground, wondering what the hell they were going to do next. They had too many skins to put them all on one boat.

"Wait for what?" McConnell asked.

Pike ignored his friend and spoke to Donna.

"What if we had a board? Could we get the damaged one off using our knives to pry it loose?"

"I guess so," she said, "but we'd have to be careful not to lose or damage the nails. We'd need them to put on a replacement . . . but we don't have a hammer."

"We could use stones to bang the nails in," Pike said. "It seems to me the only real holdup is the replacement board."

"Where are we gonna get a board?" Lobro asked.

"There are plenty of trees," Tom Gary said.

"How you gonna change a tree into a board?" Pete Styles asked.

"Wait, wait," Pike said. "Donna, couldn't we take a

board from somewhere else on the boat?"

She thought a moment and said, "We *could,* but it would have to fit perfectly. We don't have the equipment to saw it if it's too big."

"Let's worry about that when the time comes. Can we pry the board off without sinking the boat?"

"We'd have to bring it into shallow water."

"We can do that," Pike said. "There are enough of us to free it if it gets caught on the bottom."

"Wait a second," McConnell said. "So we pry the bad board loose. What do we use to replace it?"

"Leave that to Donna and me," Pike said. "You fellas just get the boat into shallow water and pry off that board."

"And be careful of the nails," Donna said as she was being pulled by the hand by Pike.

While the others hauled the boat into shallow water and set about to pry the board loose, Pike and Donna boarded the other mackinaw.

"What we need is a board the right size, right?" he asked.

"Right."

"Couldn't we use one of the boards that was used for the floor?"

"You mean the deck?"

"Yeah, the deck, the floor, whatever," Pike said. "It isn't going to hurt the boat to have one board less in the deck, is it?"

"Well . . . no."

"So all we have to do is measure the damaged board up against these floorboards—uh, deck boards—and find one the right size."

"And then pry it up."

"We can do that," Pike said.

"You know," she said, looking at him, "if we find a board the right size, I think we can do this."

"It's worth a try," Pike said. "Hell, it's worth a helluva lot *more* than a try."

Once McConnell and the others had the damaged board loose, Pike had a couple of the men go and look for flat stones they could use as hammers.

"Did you get all the nails?" Donna asked.

"Uh, we got most of them," McConnell said.

"What do you mean by most?" she asked.

"We dropped one into the water, and bent two other ones."

"Damn!"

"Forget it," Pike said. "We can do without one nail, and we can use the same flat rocks to straighten out the bent ones. We're going to do this, people!"

Donna looked at McConnell and said, "He's got me believing it."

"Hell," McConnell said, "I *always* believe him, no matter what kind of schemes he comes up with."

"Ha!" Pike said. "Spoken by the king of harebrained schemes."

Pike picked up the board and said to Donna, "Come on, we'll find one the right size, and we might as well take it off of Skins's boat. He's the one who damaged it."

"Me?"

"If you could steer—"

211

"If I could steer?" McConnell said. "Tell that to Donna?"

"What?"

"She jumped up and grabbed the tiller when things got really bad," McConnell said. "She helped me steer right into that wall!"

Donna cleared her throat and said to Pike, "Let's get started looking for that board."

"Skins," Pike said, "see what you can do about straightening out those nails."

"Right."

Pike looked at Donna, shook his head, and said, "Women steerers."

Pike and Donna climbed aboard McConnell's mackinaw and started measuring the damaged board up against the boards of the deck.

"Hey," Mike Collins called.

"What?" Pike said.

"Is there somethin' goin' on that I should know about?" he asked, sounding worried.

"Don't worry," Pike said. "We're just fixing the boat so it won't sink."

"We're sinkin'," he said, "and you guys left me here alone?"

"We're not sinkin', Mike," Donna said.

"Well then, what the hell—"

"Just go to sleep, Collins," Pike growled. "We'll wake you if we sink."

"We're in luck," she said. "The builder used the same size boards on the hull as he did on the deck."

"Then we can use one?"

"Sure," she said, "just pick one you like."

"Uh, which one can the boat do without the most?" he asked.

She just waved her hand and said, "Take one from the bow. We don't want Skins steppin' in a hole while he's steering."

Pike got down on his hands and knees and started prying up a board with his knife.

"Hey," he said, "we get some extra nails with this, too."

"Fine," she said. "We'll put them to use. When we put this board on the hull, it's not going to be as sound as it was."

"Why not?"

"It just isn't," she said. "It ain't the original board, and the nails have been pried loose once and reused. It just ain't gonna be as strong."

Pike looked up at her and said, "But it will hold, won't it?"

"Yeah," she said, "of course it will hold. . . ."

"Good."

". . . For a while."

While Pike pried up the board they would use as a replacement, McConnell knelt on the shore and used two flat rocks to straighten out the bent nails. He laid them on one rock and hammered them with the other until they were reasonably straight. By the time he was done, though, the rocks he had used were cracked.

"We need stronger rocks than these," he told the others. "Let's look around."

In the end they got rocks that weren't totally flat, and

were thicker than the ones he had used. He carried them out to the boat, with the nails in his other hand.

"The board has to bend," Donna said to Pike as McConnell reached them. Pike and Donna were on the side of the boat, holding the replacement board up to the hole it had to fit in.

"It's too long," Pike said.

"It's *not* too long," she said. "It has to bend. The bow is *curved."*

"If I bend it it'll break."

"Well, *bend* it, don't *break* it!" she said.

"All right!"

"Uh, I've got the stones and nails," McConnell said.

"Skins," Pike said, "give me a hand."

"Don't stop the nails . . ." Donna said.

"Here . . . you take the nails . . . and the stones . . . "

"I've got them. . . ."

"Skins, grab the top and hold it tight while I bend the bottom . . ."

"Don't break it, for God's sake!" Donna said.

"I'm *trying* not to. . . ." Pike said.

"Watch it. . . ."

"Keep quiet while I do this. . . ."

"I'll keep quiet if you do it right. . . ."

CHAPTER TWENTY-SEVEN

It took a long time, but they finally got the board in place. Pike hurt a couple of fingers pounding on the nails with a stone, and when McConnell moved in to relieve him, he did the same.

When they looked at Donna she shook her head and held her hands out in front of her.

"I'm the supervisor," she said. "I'm not mashin' *my* fingers."

Pike and McConnell continued taking turns holding the board and banging the nails, and finally got all the nails into place.

When they were finished they stood back to regard their handiwork.

"How does it look?" Pike asked Donna.

"How it looks don't matter," Donna said. "What matters is if it holds."

"The only place we're gonna find that out is on the water," McConnell said.

"And we'll do just that," Pike said, "in the morning. This boat repairing is hard work."

"Yeah," McConnell said, "I could use some rest and some food, too."

"Me, too!" a voice called from the boat. "Are you guys finished banging on the boat?"

"We're all done, Collins," Pike said.

"And you ain't sinkin'," McConnell said.

"Come on," Donna said. "I'll do the cookin' tonight. The last time one of you guys cooked I was still chewin' the next day."

"That wasn't me," McConnell said. "I can cook."

"*You* can cook?" Pike said, as the three of them started back to shore. "I'm the one who always does the cooking."

"You? That's a laugh. . . ."

When they reached shore they told the others that the work on the boat was done.

"Will it float?" Pat Lobro asked.

"Why don't you fellas go out there and push it back into the deep water, so we can see," Pike said.

"And if it starts to sink," McConnell said, "make sure you get Collins off of it."

"It won't sink," Pike said. "That boat is as good as new."

Donna gave him a baleful look, and he said, "Okay, so it's *not* as good as new, it's *almost* as good as new."

"We'll see . . ." she said.

They watched while six of the men put their shoulders into the side of the boat, forcing it loose from the bottom and floating it back out onto the river. On shore the rest of the men were holding onto the lines so the boat wouldn't get caught up in the current. Donna

216

watched while she threw some bacon and beans into a frying pan, and put on another pot of coffee.

The boat started to float on its own, so Lobro, Styles, and the others backed off. On shore the men holding the ropes—John Blackburn and Pike among them, because they were the two biggest men—retied them so that the boat was secured.

"It's floating," McConnell said.

"Check the other side," Pike called out. "Where we made the repair."

The six men had a conversation, and Lobro apparently lost out. He took off his shirt and swam around to the other side of the boat. After a few moments, he swam back around and waded in, holding his shirt.

"It doesn't look like it's takin' any water," Lobro said.

"Let's hope it stays that way," Pike said. "We'll have to watch it overnight and then see how it looks in the morning."

"It'll look fine," Donna said. "Right now why don't you fellas come and eat."

They gathered round her so she could spoon out the dinner, and then they all found their own spots to sit and eat, in twos or threes. Blackburn went off and sat by himself.

"I think this is the first time he's gonna eat since we got on those boats," McConnell said to Pike.

"Well, he hasn't gotten in the way yet," Pike said, "so leave him alone."

Pike was trying to hold his plate in the hand with the two injured fingers. He finally decided just to put the plate down on his lap. Luckily, there wasn't anything

217

that needed to be cut, and he didn't have to hold a knife.

McConnell had banged one finger, but it didn't seem to be getting in his way.

"What do you think?" McConnell asked.

"About what?"

"Are we being watched right now?"

Pike shrugged.

"It doesn't feel like it?"

"Then what's Devers's plan?" McConnell asked.

"Well," Pike said, "he could be ahead of us, waiting for us."

"But where?"

"Someplace that's perfect for an ambush," Pike said.

"It's too bad we don't have a couple of horses," McConnell said. "We could just ride ahead and check out the other bends in the river."

"Well," Pike said, "We don't have to go through another steep gorge like that last one. Repairs may not be so easy next time."

"This was easy?" McConnell asked, holding up his swollen thumb.

As with the night before, Pike couldn't sleep. This time, however, McConnell had no trouble dropping off. Instead of making Donna stay on the boat with Collins, Pike let her bed down on shore. Tom Gary stayed on the boat with the injured man.

Pike was sitting nursing a cup of coffee when Donna came walking up to him.

"Mind a little company?" she asked.

"Nope," he said, "not your kind. Pull up a piece of the ground."

She sat cross-legged on the ground next to him and he handed her a cup of coffee.

"Oooh," she said after she sipped it, "this isn't mine."

"No," Pike said, "yours all went. I made this pot."

"Maybe Skins was right," she said, putting the cup aside.

"About my cooking?" he asked. "You should taste his coffee."

"No thanks."

"There's some bacon left," he said. "It's cold."

"That's okay," she said, taking the plate he handed her with the cold, dried-up pieces of bacon. She munched on them in small bites.

"At this rate we'll never get where we're goin'," she said.

"Maybe it'll be clear going from here on in," Pike said.

"You don't really believe that, do you?" she asked. "I mean, you're still expectin' Cal Devers to try somethin', right?"

He looked at her and said, "Yes, I am."

She hunched her shoulders against the cold night air and said, "He's sure makin' us wait."

"That's his game."

"It's a game?"

"He acts like it is," Pike said, "and he always likes to come out on top."

"Don't you?"

"There's a difference," Pike said. "I don't kill people to do it."

There was a moment of hesitation, and then she said, "No, I guess you don't."

She popped the last piece of bacon into his mouth, then wiped her hands on her thighs.

"I guess I'll try to get some sleep."

"Do that," he said. "Try not to worry."

"About what? That someone will come and try to kill me in my sleep?"

She went over to her blanket, lay down, and pulled it over herself. Pike guessed she was having second thoughts about hitching herself to their wagon—not that he could blame her. She wanted to get to St. Louis, but she didn't want to risk her life doing it.

Pike looked down at the two sore fingers on his left hand. They were still swollen and stiff, but they didn't hurt as much. He made a fist, then flexed his hand. If he needed to use his rifle, the fingers weren't going to affect his accuracy.

Pike turned and looked at the darkness behind him. This wouldn't be a bad time for Devers and his men to make their move, while most of them were asleep. Of course, Pike had four men on watch and one on one of the boats, watching both of them. If Devers tried, it wasn't going to be easy. No, Devers had his spot all picked out. They were just going to have to wait until they reached that spot—wherever it was.

"This is the spot," Cal Devers said.

"Here?" LeConte said, looking out at the river. "What is so special about this particular spot?"

Behind him Devers was aware that the Crow Indians, as well as Sandy Dunlap and the other white

220

men, were waiting to hear the answer. They wanted to know why they had to ride for days to get to this particular spot.

"Look out at the river," Devers said.

"I am," LeConte said.

"No," Devers said, "really look at it. Don't you notice something different?"

LeConte looked at the river. The water was flowing quickly, and there were some whiteheads that he thought shouldn't be there . . . unless . . .

"It is shallow."

"What?" Dunlap asked.

LeConte turned and looked at Dunlap.

"The water, it is shallow here. Do you see? The water turns white as it goes over the rocks."

"Very good, Henri," Devers said. "I'm impressed. There's something about the river bottom here, it slopes up. The river almost has to flow uphill."

"What's gonna happen when they get here with the boats?" Dunlap asked.

"Well," Devers said, "one of two things. Either the rocks will tear the bottom out of the boats, or they'll realize their problem and they'll have to tow the boats over the high ground."

"Tow?" one of the other men said. Devers thought it might have been the first time he heard the man— O'Brien, was it?—speak.

"Wait a minute," Dunlap said. "If those rocks tear the bottom out of the boats, they'll sink and we'll lose the skins."

"The boats can't sink, Dunlap," Devers said. "The water is too shallow. If the rocks tear up the boats, the men on it will be like sitting ducks."

"Ah," Dunlap said, "I understand."

"Good."

"What do you mean, tow?" O'Brien asked.

Devers turned and said, "They'd have to tie ropes to the front of the boats, get out and walk through the rocks, pulling the boats slowly over them so that they don't get damaged."

"Oh," O'Brien said.

"And if they have to do that," Dunlap said to O'Brien, "they'll be sitting ducks."

"Hey, Dunlap," Devers said, "you're smarter than you look."

Dunlap stared at Devers and said, "I know."

"Henri," Devers said, "you take your Indians over to the other side of the river. Whatever happens, they're gonna be at a dead stop here, and we'll be able to catch them in a cross fire."

"And then they will just be dead," LeConte said.

Devers smiled and tapped LeConte lightly on the cheek with his palm.

"You're smarter than you look, too, Henri, aren't you?"

CHAPTER TWENTY-EIGHT

They had been back on the river for about three hours when Donna turned and caught Pike's attention. He nodded for her to leave her position and join him.

"I just remembered something about this river," she said.

"What's that?"

"Someplace further on there's a place where it gets so shallow that the bottom of the boat scrapes the bottom of the river."

"Will it do damage?"

"No, but we won't be able to get over it," she said. "The last time we had to all get out, tie ropes to the front of the boat, and pull it across."

"How long a stretch is this shallow part?"

She thought a moment, then said, "I don't remember exactly. I was a lot younger then. I guess it was probably about a hundred feet."

"We have to drag these boats a hundred feet?"

"Unless something's happened over the years to that shallow stretch to change it."

223

"What else do you know about it?"

"Well, I was told that it's like a shelf, that water passed over it and under it, so that when you reach the other side the current is still strong."

"I wonder if anyone's ever tried to blast away that shelf."

"I don't know," she said. "Do you think we could?"

"I'd seriously think about it *if* we had some dynamite, which we don't."

"So what will we do?"

"I guess we'll deal with it when we come to it," he said. "Thanks for the information."

"I would have told you sooner, but I just remembered it."

"No problem."

She turned to go back to her position and he said, "Donna, how wide is this stretch?"

She frowned a moment in concentration and said, "I don't remember it as being very wide."

"Okay, thanks. Tell the others we'll be stopping for a break."

"All right."

Donna went back to her position and Pike turned and signaled to McConnell's boat that they were going in to shore.

When they were on shore McConnell said, "What's the problem?"

Pike relayed to him the information given to him by Donna.

"What are you thinkin'?" McConnell asked.

"I'm thinking that it sounds like the perfect place for

Devers and his men to make their move."

"You're right," McConnell said. "All they'd have to do is wait until we all got out of our boats to pull them, and we'd be easy targets."

"Right."

"So what do we do about it?"

"I think we'd better start walking," Pike said.

"Does Donna remember how far ahead it is?"

"No," Pike said. "I'm going to ask her to concentrate on landmarks. If she can tell us when we're approaching it, we can get out and walk on ahead before the boats and see what the situation is."

"And so what? Devers is bound to have a bunch of men. The two of us can't do much. Maybe we should take more men with us."

"Maybe," Pike said, nodding. "Maybe we should secure the boats and take everybody with us. We've got a dozen guns."

"Eleven, not counting Collins."

"Still, eleven's not bad. Devers is not going to have *too* many men, because he wouldn't want to pay out a lot of money."

"Cheap help, then," McConnell said, "and not that many. He'll probably use Indians, where he can."

"And pay them off in blankets and whiskey."

"This could work," McConnell said. "It all depends on Donna's memory, doesn't it?"

"I'm afraid so," Pike said. "I'll talk to her about it. Meanwhile, you tell the others what's going on."

"Right."

They hadn't even bothered to build a fire for coffee, because Pike didn't intend to stop for that long. He grabbed Donna and pulled her away from the others.

He asked her about landmarks.

"There might be," she admitted, "but I probably won't know until I see them—if I see them."

"We're going to have to hope you do," Pike said.

"I'll do my best."

"We can't ask any more than that, Donna," he said. "Come on, let's get back on the river."

While the others were getting back aboard the boat Pike and McConnell hung back.

"What'd they say?" Pike asked.

"If we go on foot they all want to come," McConnell said. "I think they're all anxious to get their feet firmly back on the ground again."

"Yeah," Pike said, "I think I know how they feel. I enjoyed this that first day, but since then it's been wearing out its welcome with me."

"If only we had some horses," McConnell said.

Pike turned and looked all around him, beyond the river.

"Tryin' to figure out where we are?" McConnell asked.

"Yeah."

"I can't do it, either," McConnell said. "If we knew we were near a settlement we could go and *get* some horses, but I can't locate any landmarks."

"We'll just have to keep moving," Pike said, "and rely on Donna's memory."

"I don't think we have any other choice," McConnell said.

"How's Collins's leg?"

"He says he fine," McConnell answered. "He keeps

sayin' he wants to row."

"All right, let him try," Pike said, "and put Blackburn back up front, to watch. Tell him to keep his rifle ready."

"Right," McConnell said, and then added, "that is, if he can keep from falling in."

"Tie a rope around him if you have to," Pike said.

Devers watched as Henri LeConte rode back across the river to his side. The way his horse was moving, it was obvious that the riverbed was slippery. That would work in their favor when Pike and his men got out of their boats to pull.

LeConte approached and dismounted.

"All set on the other side?" he asked.

"Oui," LeConte said, "I just wish we had given the Indians rifles."

"Sure," Devers said, "and then they wouldn't have waited around to get paid off in blankets. They would have killed us and taken off with the guns. Real smart, Henri."

"Then we should have gotten more white men—"

"Stop complaining, Henri," Devers said. "This is going to work, don't worry."

"I hope it does, *mon ami,*" LeConte said, shaking his head doubtfully.

It was late in the day, about an hour before sundown, when Donna suddenly turned her head to look at Pike. He had been watching her since noon, and her eyes had been raking the shoreline, constantly searching for

227

some sort of landmark. It was obvious now that she may have seen something.

She left her position and joined him at his.

"What is it?"

"I think we're gettin' close."

"How close?"

She looked around again, frowning and biting her bottom lip.

"Real close," she said, finally. "If we keep goin' I think we'll get to it by dark."

"That's no good," Pike said. "I want to get there before dark. We'll have to stop."

He turned and waved McConnell in to shore.

"It will be dark soon," LeConte said. "They'll have to stop and camp."

"That's no problem," Devers said. "All that means is that they'll be here bright and early in the mornin'. We can wait."

"Perhaps it would be better to find their camp and attack them at night?" LeConte said. "They would not be expecting that, would they?"

"Like I said, Henri," Devers said, folding his arms across his chest, "they'll be here nice and early tomorrow." Devers gave LeConte a hard stare that was designed to remind the Frenchman just who was in charge here.

"Like I said before," he repeated slowly, for effect, "we can wait."

CHAPTER TWENTY-NINE

There seemed to be a cloud hanging right over their camp. No one was talking, and everyone had looks on their faces like they'd lost their best friends.

"Jesus," McConnell said, "it's quiet."

Pike stopped his coffee cup just short of his mouth and said, "I think we're all wishing we had done something else for the winter."

"There's sure not gonna be as much profit in this as we all thought at the beginning of the winter."

"In the future," Pike said, "just remind me of how much trouble I get in when I deal with more than two people, will you?"

"I'll remind you if you remind me."

"What are you fellas remindin' each other about," Donna Lee asked, joining them.

She poured herself a cup of coffee while Pike told her what they had been discussing.

"Well, that makes me feel kind of guilty," she said when he was finished.

"About what?"

"I'm enjoyin' this," she said. "After all the time I spent in Fort Pierre I would have fought my way through a pack of wolves, or walked a mile over broken glass to get out. So far, this has been easy."

"So far," Pike said. "You know, I got you a rifle before we left, but we never did find out if you can shoot or not."

"Just let me have the gun," she said, "and we'll find out tomorrow."

"Yeah," McConnell said, "the hard way."

"Just what *are* we gonna do tomorrow?" Donna asked.

"Well," Pike said, "I'm thinking we should just leave the boats here and walk on ahead and see if we can't find that stretch of river you remember."

"It's there," she said. "I just don't know how far we'd have to walk from here. Also, on foot I'm not gonna see any landmarks, since I've only ever seen it from the river, and that was only once."

"I still think on foot's our best bet," Pike said. "I don't want to get caught out there on the river, which is obviously Devers's plan."

"If *we* can come up on *him* by surprise," McConnell said, "that would work much better for me."

"Me, too," Pike said.

"What about the boats?" Donna asked. "Are we just gonna leave them here alone?"

"Well," Pike said, "I thought you and Collins could stay behind and watch over them."

"Oh, no," she said, "I'm comin' with you. Remember, I'm the one who knows about that stretch of river."

"You just said you couldn't find it on foot."

"I said I *might* not be able to find it on foot," she said. "That's not the same thing."

Pike opened his mouth to argue but she jumped in ahead of him.

"You're not leavin' me behind, Jack Pike, and that's final!"

Pike looked at McConnell, who shrugged.

"All right," Pike finally said, a beaten man. "How is Collins?"

"He's been rowing well, but I don't think he'll be able to walk."

"Can we leave him behind alone?"

"I don't see why not," she said, "but it'll be up to him, won't it?"

"Yeah," Pike said, "it will."

Pike left McConnell and Donna sitting at the fire and walked over to where Collins was sitting. This was the first time since he'd been injured that they had taken him off the boat, and it had taken two men to carry him.

"How's the leg, Mike?"

Collins looked up and said, "Why lie? It hurts like hell, but I'll be all right. I'm lucky it didn't hit a bone, might've broken it."

"Or it might have splintered the arrow," Pike said. "There would have been a lot of tiny pieces of wood in there that would never come out."

"Like I said," Collins said, "I was lucky."

"I've got to ask you something, Mike, and you're going to be the one who makes the final decision."

"Go ahead," Collins said.

Pike outlined his plan, that he and others would go ahead on foot, and Collins would stay behind with the

231

boats, well armed.

"Well armed or not, if more than three people stumble onto me, I'm done."

"I could leave more men with you—"

"No," Collins said, "the same thing would apply. If you leave two, we're in trouble if we have to go against six, and on and on. No, I'll be fine—just don't stay away too long. I'm not gonna be able to go anywhere by myself without a horse, and I don't think I can take one of these mackinaws downriver alone."

"You're sure?" Pike asked.

"Hey," Collins said, "go do what you gotta do, Pike. I'll be fine."

Pike put his hand on the man's shoulder and said, "Thanks, Mike. We'll be back as soon as we can."

"Why don't you come back in about ten seconds," Collins said, extending his cup, "with another cup of coffee?"

Pike grinned and took the cup. He got the man another cup of coffee, then went back to sit with McConnell and Donna.

"He'll be okay," Pike said. "Skins, why don't you tell the others that we'll be getting an early start in the morning . . . on foot?"

"Right."

Left alone, Donna poured another cup of coffee for Pike and handed it to him.

"I hope you're right, Donna."

"Oh," she said, rolling her eyes, "don't put any pressure on me. Seriously, I hope I'm right, too. I don't want us walking for miles and not finding anything."

Pike looked up as someone approached, thinking it would be McConnell. It was Pat Lobro.

232

"Pat," Pike said.

"More coffee?" Donna asked.

"No, thanks," Lobro said. "Skins just told us what you're plannin' for tomorrow."

"Do you have any ideas, Pat?"

"Yeah, I do," Lobro said. "Actually, Pete Styles and I do."

Pike nodded and said, "Go ahead, then."

"Pete and I figure if we leave tonight, we'll be able to cover a lot more ground with just the two of us. By the time you leave tomorrow, we may already know what we have to know."

"Are you suggesting that we all wait here while the two of you go ahead?"

"No, that's not what we mean," Lobro said. "We just want to start out now. We'll probably meet you along the way when we start back."

"What will that accomplish?"

"A couple of things," Lobro said. "We may come across Devers and his men while it's still dark. Since it's just the two of us, we'll be able to get closer and really take a look at the situation."

"You have a point."

"Also, if we don't find anything, we can keep the rest of you from walkin' all that way for nothin'."

Pike looked at Donna, who nodded.

"Okay," Pike said. "If the two of you are willing, I don't see any problems with it."

"Good," Lobro said.

"You want to take some food?"

"No," Lobro said, "all we'll take are our guns. We wanna travel light."

"Good idea."

233

Lobro nodded and said, "Thanks," and went to tell Styles. He passed McConnell along the way, to whom he nodded.

"You agreed?"

"Sure, why not? It'll probably do them more good, too, than staying here overnight."

"They're anxious to get movin', but nobody more than Lobro and Styles," McConnell said.

"They're good men," Pike said.

"They're all good men, Pike."

"Yeah," Pike said. "It's the good ones that men like Devers manage to hurt."

"Maybe not this time," Donna said.

"No," Pike said, "not this time, not if I have anything to say about it."

Pat Lobro and Pete Styles collected their rifles and possibles bags and were wished good luck by all the rest of the men. Pike watched them walk off and melt away into the darkness.

When the two of them were gone the others all settled down with their blankets and fell asleep—all but Pike, that is. More tonight than any other night he didn't feel like sleeping.

He wondered if he'd ever feel like sleeping again until they had all the goods delivered, and he was finished with this whole business.

CHAPTER THIRTY

Lobro and Styles were in their element, even in the dark. A ride down the river was nice, but there was nothing like having your feet on firm ground.

Both men had spent years in the mountains, and moving around in the dark was no problem for them. Although they were unfamiliar with the area, their instincts allowed them to move swiftly and surely through the darkness.

They traveled without rest, moving as quietly as they could. There was no telling when they would stumble onto someone, and they didn't want to be heard coming. Staying quiet included not talking, but they had been friends and partners for so long they didn't need to talk.

It was that longtime friendship, and those ingrained instincts, that caused them both to stop walking at the same time, even before Lobro put his hand on Styles's arm.

*****

At first light Pike woke up. That was the first time he realized that he had fallen asleep. He sat up and looked around, but no one else was up. He moved around camp, waking them.

"Coffee?" Donna asked.

"Yes," Pike said, "but make it fast."

He figured they'd all move better with something warm in their stomachs—for a while, anyway.

Pike had three men carry some food and coffee, just in case they needed it. Of course, their intention was to return as soon as possible, but anything could happen.

They left Mike Collins his rifle and Pike's Kentucky pistol, as well as food, water, and coffee, and they moved him over near the fire, where he'd be warm. One of the men went off and found him a large tree branch that he could use as a crutch if he had to get around.

They considered leaving him on one of the boats, but decided against it. He'd be helpless to get back to the riverbank if he had to. He was better off on dry land to start with.

Donna checked his leg one more time before they left, changing the bandage, and then they started off with Pike in the lead and McConnell bringing up the rear. Donna walked up front with Pike, her eyes alert for landmarks.

They were all tense, because for the first time since they had started downriver, they were looking forward to some sort of confrontation with other men, rather than just with the river.

Pike wondered how far Lobro and Styles had gotten during the night, and what—if anything—they had managed to find out.

Cal Devers thought he could sense Henri LeConte's nervousness even from across the river. The Frenchman was all alone as a tracker, but his nerve left something to be desired. He loved tracking people, but hated finding them. Devers just hoped he would react well when the time came, and keep the Indians under control.

On his side of the river Devers sensed only eagerness from the men with him. Dunlap and the others liked this sort of thing so much they probably would have done it *without* being paid.

Devers was also eager. He wanted to see that lead boat coming down the river with Pike acting as steersman. He knew that a man like Pike *would* be riding in the lead boat. He'd wait, though, until they were all out of the boats. Those were the orders everyone had. Nobody fires until everyone is out of the boats and standing in the river. When the shooting started, none of Pike's people would be able to get a firm foothold, and that would work in Devers's favor. By the time they knew what hit them, half of them would be dead, and the rest as good as. Then all they'd have to do was move in and collect the goods.

Devers hated taking the goods to market with the mackinaws. He favored mules, and he had plenty of them nearby. The men he was getting the mules from were being paid for the animals, rather than cut in on the deal. The delivery of the mules was part of the service. Once they had the skins loaded on the mules, they'd pay off the Indians and get rid of them—unless he decided they were better off killing the savages. That decision would wait until he saw what happened after they finished with Pike and his people.

The time when those goods would be his was getting closer, and Devers did this sort of thing for the feeling he was experiencing now, almost as much as he did it for the profit.

There was something special about taking something that didn't belong to you away from the person or people it *did* belong to.

Lobro and Styles met up with each other again on Lobro's side of the river after Styles went across to see what he could see.

"It's like we thought," he said. "They've got both sides of the river covered."

"So we'd be caught in a cross fire when we got out to pull the boats," Lobro said. "Devers knew about this all along."

"Looks like it," Styles said. "The other side has about six or eight Crow Indians and one white man."

"We've got about seven white men on this side. One of them has to be Devers."

"Okay," Devers said, "so we've got what we need. Let's go meet up with Pike and the others."

"Too bad we don't know which one is Devers," Lobro said.

"What are you thinkin'?"

"If we killed Devers," Lobro said, "maybe the others would scatter."

Styles thought it over and then shook his head.

"No, Pat, let's stick to the original plan," he said, finally. "We'll be better off with the others backin' us up."

"Okay," Lobro said, "okay, then let's go."

"Wait," Pike said. He stopped and everyone behind him stopped. McConnell came up to stand next to him.

"What is it?" Donna asked.

"I hear something."

She listened and said, "I don't hear anything."

"Shh," McConnell said.

They waited, and before long two men came into view, coming toward them.

Lobro and Styles.

CHAPTER THIRTY-ONE

They met up on a rocky incline, and retraced their steps until they reached a clearing that was more suitable for them to talk.

Lobro did the talking, explaining that they had come up on Devers's camp halfway through the night.

"Their fires gave them away," he explained.

"Fires?" Pike asked. "More than one? They have that many men that they needed more than one fire?"

"Two camps," Lobro said, "one on each side of the river."

"They've got about six to eight men on each side," Styles said. "Sixteen men at the most, a dozen at the least."

"Not bad odds," Pike said, "considering we're eleven strong. How are they armed?"

"Rifles," Lobro said.

"There are Indians on the other side of the river, and they don't have rifles."

"That's even better."

"You'd think Devers would have given them rifles,"

Tom Gary said.

"He couldn't risk it," Pike said, understanding the man's position. "He couldn't take the chance that the Indians would turn on him with the rifles." He turned to Lobro and asked, "How far ahead of us are they?"

"A couple of hours at the most."

"All right," Pike said. "Let's push on. With a little luck we can have this wrapped up before dark."

One way or the other, he thought.

Lobro and Styles took the lead, with Pike and Donna right behind them. Since they knew the way, they might even close the gap between themselves and Devers's camp in less than two hours.

As the time went by the eagerness in all of them grew, until it was an almost tangible thing hanging in the air above them.

After almost two hours Lobro and Styles called them to a halt.

"We can separate here," Lobro said. "Some of us can swim over to the other side of the river."

"Who are the best swimmers?" Pike asked. Whoever volunteered to swim across was going to have to do so while trying to keep their rifles and powder dry while fighting the current. That would take a good swimmer.

Tom Gary stepped forward with Pete Styles and Skins McConnell. Joe Rand also volunteered, with Matt Christopher. That left Pike with Lobro, Paul Exman, Wally Dennis, Donna, and Blackburn.

"Follow me," Styles said, and the volunteer swimmers did so.

"Keep your powder dry," Pike said, and McConnell waved.

"All right," Pike said to Lobro, "it's your call. You

know how long it will take Styles and the others to reach the other side."

"Right," Lobro said. "I'll say when. . . ."

Styles led McConnell and the others to the riverbank, where they moved into the water. The current was strong, but all five men were good swimmers. It was awkward, trying to swim while holding their rifles and powder out of the water, but finally they reached the other side and followed Styles to a position behind some rocks.

"Any chance we were seen from downriver?" McConnell asked.

"No," Styles said, "there's a small bend further down that would keep us hidden."

"All right, then," McConnell said. Like the others he was wet and shivering, but they had no time to let the sun dry them. "Lead on, Pete."

"This way . . ." Styles said.

"All right," Lobro said.

"Are you sure?" Pike asked.

"They should be in position by now," Lobro assured him.

Pike shrugged and said, "Okay, then, lead the way, Pat."

"There," Styles said, pointing, "see them?"

"I see them," McConnell said.

They had left the other three behind and moved

ahead, so Styles could show McConnell where the Indians and the one white man were positioned. When McConnell saw the white man he recognized him.

"That's the Frenchman from Fort Pierre," he told Styles.

"Then Devers is on the other side," Styles said.

"With Pike," McConnell said. "Let's get back to the others."

They turned and went back to where Rand, Christopher, and Gary were waiting.

"When do we go in?" Gary asked.

"That's up to Styles," McConnell said. "He and Lobro are gonna have to call it."

"No problem," Styles said. "Any minute now . . ."

Devers finished his coffee and tossed the remnants into the fire. He had Dunlap on the riverbank, watching for the boats. There was a bend upriver, but they should still have plenty of time once Dunlap spotted the boats to get into position. Still, he decided to walk up to the riverbank himself, just to have a quick look.

Pike followed Lobro ahead while the others waited behind. As soon as he came within sight of the camp he saw Cal Devers. It was the first time since they discovered that someone was following them that he was dead sure that Devers was behind it.

"Devers," he whispered.

"Which one?" Lobro asked.

"The dark-haired one sitting by the fire," Pike said.

"He's getting up, now."

They watched as Devers rose and then started walking toward the river.

"Not a very big man, is he?" Lobro asked. He looked at Pike, daring him to say something.

"No," Pike said, simply, "he's not. Let's get back to the others."

When they reached the others Blackburn asked, "How are we gonna play this?"

"We're *not* playing," Pike said. "We're going to go into camp and we're going to start shooting. By the time we're done, I don't want any of them standing."

"Without warning?" Exman asked.

"What they had planned for us would have been without warning, too, Paul," Pike said. "You still want to give them a chance?"

"No," Exman said, shaking his head.

"Anyone else object?"

They all shook their heads.

"What do we do if some of them start running?" Blackburn asked.

"Don't chase them," Pike said. "If they want to go, let them go."

"The others know all this?" Wally Dennis asked.

"Skins knows. . . ." Pike said.

He and McConnell had discussed what they would do when they finally caught with the Devers and his men. They decided that the only way to handle the situation was with deadly force. Either kill Devers and his men, or scatter them so they couldn't do any damage. Actually, it was Pike's idea, but McConnell agreed readily enough.

"You want Devers, Pike?" Lobro asked. "Want us to

save him for you?"

"I said we're not playing games, here. Whoever gets him gets him," Pike said. "This is not something personal, and playing it like it was could get somebody killed." He looked at them all and said, "If you get him in your sights, take the shot. Understand?"

They all indicated that they understood.

"All right, Pat," Pike said to Lobro, "just say when. . . ."

CHAPTER THIRTY-TWO

Nobody was really aware of anything until the first shots. . . .

When the first shots came it was almost simultaneous with Styles saying, "All right, let's go."

As a matter of fact, the way McConnell remembered it later, the shots actually drowned out the word *go* at the end of Styles's sentence.

Henri LeConte heard the shots across the river and wondered what was going on. He didn't see any boats on the river.

What had gone wrong, he wondered, and then suddenly, even before he heard the shot, he felt a pain in his back, and knew that something had gone very, very wrong.

He opened his mouth to call out Devers's name, but blood came out instead. . . .

The Indians, who were looking to LeConte for their signal, were confused when they saw him fall. By the time they realized that something was wrong, Styles, McConnell, and the others were on them, first firing their rifles, and then reversing them and using them as clubs.

Devers was down by the river when he heard the shots. They came from behind, and he knew immediately that he had been outflanked. He should have set watches other than the ones on the river. Well, it was too late to worry about that now. His men had been surprised, and now he heard the shots from across the river, as well. There was only one thing for him to do.

He jumped in the river.

As Pike and the others charged into the camp, firing their weapons, Pike saw Devers down by the river. The man didn't even hesitate when the shooting started. He jumped in the river and started swimming with the current.

"Pat—" he shouted, but Lobro had also seen Devers dive into the water.

"Go!" he shouted.

Pike took off on a run, not even stopping to reload. He ran parallel with the river, and saw Devers swimming just ahead of him. The current was carrying the man along at a good pace, but Pike's legs were long, and he wanted Devers enough to run as long as the river did.

Keeping Devers in sight, he saw that the man was now changing his course. The current was still taking him, but he had started to angle across to the other side of the river. From what Pike could see, the man had both hands in the water. He either didn't have a gun, or it was good and wet by now.

Pike discarded his own rifle and jumped into the river. He had to swim as hard as he could to get to the other side and not lose too much ground on Devers, who would make it across first. The current carried him downriver as he swam across, which would work in his favor by keeping him closer to Devers.

He saw Devers reach the other side and scramble up on the riverbank. For a moment the man looked as if he wanted to rest, but then he turned and saw Pike in the water, and started running.

When Pike's feet touched firm ground he pushed himself out of the river and ran after Devers.

It was a footrace now, and Pike had a clear advantage in that department. The smaller man was no match for Pike's long strides.

Pike was closing ground on Devers, even as they scrambled over rocks and bushes, until suddenly Devers turned with a Kentucky pistol in his hand, and pointed it at Pike.

"Stop right there, Pike!" Devers gasped. The man was fighting for air.

"I knew it was you, Devers," Pike said.

"Yeah? You knew, huh? Did you also know that I'd end up killing you?"

"Not with that pistol," Pike said.

"Why not?"

"The powder's all wet, Devers," Pike said. "If you weren't so desperate you'd realize that."

The realization did dawn on Devers then. Pike saw it

in his eyes. The man pulled the trigger and the gun clicked hollowly. Devers immediately reversed the weapon and ran at Pike, intending to use it as a club.

As he swung at Pike the bigger man sidestepped and hit Devers in the stomach. Devers's momentum kept him going a few feet before he went sprawling on all fours. The useless gun went clattering away.

Pike turned and waited for Devers to get up.

"Remember Tom Seidman, Devers?"

"Who?" Devers gasped, trying to get to his feet.

"Seidman!" Pike shouted. "You slit his throat and stole his skins—*my* skins."

"I don't remember no Seidman," Devers gasped, "and if you lost some skins, you can't prove—"

Pike stepped forward and stopped Devers by hitting him in the face. The man was down on his back, spitting blood from his cut mouth.

"You were going to ambush me and my people, weren't you, Devers? Kill us all, was that the idea?"

"You can't prove nothin'," Devers said. He was lisping, because he had swallowed a couple of front teeth. "I ain't goin to jail on thomethin' you can't prove."

"I ain't sendin' you to jail, Devers," Pike said. "I'm giving you a much shorter sentence then that."

"Wha—what are you talkin' about—" Devers said. Blood was dripping down his chin, and he was fighting to focus his eyes.

Pike reached down, grabbed the man by the shirtfront and hauled him to his feet.

"You've got time to remember Tom Seidman, Devers," Pike said. "And you have time to regret trying to ambush me. You've got as long as it takes for me to beat you to death with my bare hands."

"Wha—" Devers said, but Pike hit him again, this time holding him up so he couldn't fall . . . and then he hit him again . . . and again . . .

By the time Pike returned to camp everyone was on the camp side of the river. The ground was littered with the bodies of Devers's men. McConnell approached him, a look of concern in his eyes. Donna was right behind him, with the same look.

"Are you all right?" McConnell asked him.

Pike nodded. He was dripping wet, holding his rifle in his left hand. McConnell noticed that both hands were bleeding around the knuckles.

"What happened?"

". . . how did things go here . . . ?" Pike asked, breathlessly.

"Most of Devers's men are dead," McConnell said. "A couple of the Indian ran off. We didn't chase them. We've got two men who are still alive. One of them is Sandy Dunlap. Remember him?"

". . . hired gun . . ." Pike said, still out of breath. He hadn't even noticed how out of breath he was until he started back. He wasn't even out of breath from the running or swimming . . . it was the other thing . . . "Hired muscle . . . I remember him . . ."

"What should we do with Dunlap and the other man?" McConnell asked.

Pike waved one hand weakly and said, "Let them go . . . can't do any damage . . ."

McConnell turned and called out to Pat Lobro to let Dunlap and the other man go, then he looked back at his friend with concern.

"Do you want to sit down?" McConnell asked.

Pike shook his head.

"Are you sure you're all right?" Donna asked.

". . . be all right . . . in a minute . . ." Pike said.

"What happened to your hands?" Donna asked. She reached out as if to touch him, but stopped short.

Pike didn't answer.

"Where's Devers, Pike?" McConnell asked. "Did he get away?"

Pike looked down at one bleeding hand, and closed it into a painful fist. Then he looked at his friend.

"No, Skins," Pike said, "he didn't get away."

McConnell stared at Pike for a moment, then realized what his friend meant.

"Jesus, Pike . . ."

Pike ran his bloody hand over his face and said, "I'm not proud of it."

"Proud of what?" Donna asked. "What happened?"

Neither man answered.

"Pike?" she said. "What happened?"

Pike looked at her, opened his mouth to speak, and then thought better of it. What could he say to her? How could he describe to her the savage, uncontrollable anger he had felt when face-to-face with Devers? How could he tell her what he'd done?

"You tell her, Skins," he said, finally, walking past both of them. "You tell her . . ."

EPILOGUE

They went back to retrieve the boats, pulled them across the shelf with ropes, and then continued downriver until they reached the port of St. Louis.

Donna had taken the time to wrap Pike's hands, but she didn't speak to him. Word of what he had done spread to the others, who looked at him in a new light after that. It takes a special kind of man, and an ugly kind of anger, to make him beat another man to death with his bare hands. It was not something any of them could really identify with, except maybe McConnell. He had seen that kind of anger in his friend before, but he didn't like it any more this time than he had the other times.

When they reached St. Louis, Pike left it to McConnell and the others to sell the skins, as well as the mackinaws. He found a saloon right on the port and drank beer until he couldn't lift his head anymore.

When Pike woke he looked around him. He was in a

bed, in a hotel room. Obviously, someone had brought him here from the saloon.

He sat up and was surprised that he didn't feel a hangover. Naked, he looked around, located his clothes and got dressed. He went downstairs and found McConnell in the hotel dining room, sitting alone.

"Are you all in one piece?" McConnell asked as Pike sat across from him.

"I guess."

"Want some breakfast?"

"Is it morning?"

"Yes."

"Then I'll have some breakfast."

McConnell called the waiter over and ordered the same thing for Pike that he had for himself, steak and eggs. He then poured Pike some coffee.

"The goods all sold?" Pike asked.

"Yep," McConnell said, "I have our share."

"Where is everybody?"

"Most of them wanted to see St. Louis before they left."

"Not me," Pike said, "I've seen St. Louis."

"So have I," McConnell said. "I bought us two horses. Figured we'd get an early start."

"Good idea," Pike said. "Right after breakfast."

"Right."

They drank coffee for a while and then the waiter came with their food.

"Where's Donna?" Pike finally asked.

"She's staying here," McConnell said. "She went to find a place to work, and a place to live."

"Uh-huh."

"She, uh, said she didn't want to see you."

"Sure."

"That's not somethin' a woman can deal with easily, Pike," McConnell said. "That kind of anger—that kind of reaction to anger—"

"I understand," Pike said.

"Are you all right?"

"I'm fine," Pike said. "It was like the last time, Skins, with Sun Rising? When I hunted the men who killed her? I had no control. I kept seeing Tom Seidman's face, above that gaping wound in his throat . . ."

"I know," McConnell said.

"You ever get that angry, Skins?"

After a moment McConnell said, "Uh, no, Pike, I never have."

They finished breakfast and had another cup of coffee each, then called the waiter over and paid for the food.

"Ready to go back to the mountains?" McConnell asked.

Pike nodded and said, "More than ready, Skins, to go back . . . *high* into the mountains, where there are no people."